D0559463

WITHDRAWN HEDBERG LIBRARY

GIFT OF

John Warren Stewig

Carthage

Three Sisters

Cur
PZ
7
m4739 8
Th
1986

Three Sisters

Norma Fox Mazer

**SCHOLASTIC
HARDCOVER**

Scholastic Inc.
New York

HEDBERG LIBRARY
CARTHAGE COLLEGE
KENOSHA, WISCONSIN

Copyright © 1986 by Norma Fox Mazer. All rights reserved. Published by Scholastic Inc.

No part of this publication may be reproduced in whole or in part, or stored in a retrieval system, or transmitted in any form or by any means, electronic, mechanical, photocopying, recording, or otherwise, without written permission of the publisher. For information regarding permission, write to Scholastic Inc., 730 Broadway, New York, NY 10003.

Library of Congress Cataloging-in-Publication Data

Mazer, Norma Fox
Three sisters.

Summary: Karen's misplaced romantic feelings for her sister Liz's boyfriend threaten to alienate Karen, but a disturbing revelation from the third sister in the family promises to bind them all together again.
[1. Sisters–Fiction] I. Title
PZ7.M47398Th 1986   [Fic]   85-22133
ISBN 0-590-33774-2

12 11 10 9 8 7 6 5 4 3 2 1   2   6 7 8 9/8 0 1/9

Printed in the U.S.A.

HEGGERG LIBRARY
CARTHAGE COLLEGE
KENOSHA, WISCONSIN

For Margie Lewis—
for friendship, laughter, and books.

In the cold silky wash of the moon across the water she heard her sisters calling her. Karen. Karen. Kaaaaaren. . . .

She swam strongly, plunging in and out of the dark, thick water, her arms stroking, clearing the way, her head coming up slick and playful for a mouthful of moon cold air.

Kaaaaren. . . .

In and out . . . in and out. . . . She could swim on forever in this moon silky water, her sisters' voices falling like water over her. Karen, oh, Karen, come back, Karen, come baaack. . . .

They were both there on the shore, the shore all white sand stretching for empty miles, and she saw them, saw her sisters in their finery, dressed for a party. Then she was running after them, the sand pulling at her feet. They were going somewhere, going away, going to some wonderful place without her. Wait for me, wait for me. Liz, Tobi. . . . Wait . . . wait . . . wait.

One

Sisters. Her sisters. Always her sisters. Her first memory: a sister, holding her by the hand, pulling her down the street. "Come on, baby." And this memory and all the memories pull her down the years. There are three of them and they are each three years apart. They are Liz, Tobi, and herself, Karen. They are twenty-one, eighteen, and fifteen.

Twenty-one works. Eighteen goes to college. Fifteen to high school. There are still times when they get together, sprawl on Liz's bed, eat popcorn and apples, and talk half the night. Tobi, middle sister, will argue about anything. Liz sits cross-legged, calm, a golden Buddha. Karen looks from one to the other, excited by the three of them being together.

Their mother pokes her head in the door. "What are you girls talking about so long?" She smiles at them as if to say, "Can't I join you?" They yawn and say harmless things about the weather. She leaves and Tobi raises a finger for silence until they're sure they're alone. Then they start again. "Mom doesn't have any women friends," Liz says.

One of the sisters' favorite things is analyzing their parents: their relationship, their characters, their failings. Their mother is a librarian, their father a dentist; the sisters agree that these are the safe professions, nothing risky, nothing really exciting or creative. They agree that their parents are strange: On the one hand, they each go their own way; on the other, they're close to one another. Too close?

"They love us, sure," Tobi says, "but you can tell they're more important to each other. Dad turns to Mom for everything."

"I don't think that's so bad," Liz says.

"No, he can't even buy a pair of socks without —"

"But that's so touching, actually."

Tobi gags. "Save me from a man like that."

Karen wants to contribute to this. "You know, they never let us hear them fight."

Tobi's eyebrows draw together. "I always wanted them, Mom especially, to pay more attention to me."

"How about Dad?" Karen says.

"He's sorta sweet." Liz rocks back and forth, pats the top of her head, hums. Tobi and Karen snicker. Dad to a T. In the office he's Mr. Crisp, wears whites, probes his patients' mouths with pink hands and shining fingernails. At home, though, it's baggy pants, shirts with missing buttons. At the table, he invariably tips back in his chair, patting the bald spot on his head, humming to himself. Lost in his own space.

"All his life he's been in training to be a character," Tobi says.

Karen wishes she'd said that.

"And considering Grandma," Tobi goes on, "it's no wonder!"

"Come on," Liz says in her slow drawl, "we're not such a baaad family. You only have to look at other families —"

"Too true," Tobi rushes in. "The junk that goes on! I'm not talking Mickey Mouse stuff. I mean really terrible things. Beatings. Incest. Did you see that story in the paper about the man who kept his daughter locked in a box?"

Karen thinks how intense Tobi is, how deeply Tobi feels everything. Is *she* intense? Does she feel things enough?

"I'm not talking room," Tobi says. "I mean an actual box. For six years he kept her in a box. She couldn't walk when the police found her."

Liz shudders, taps her lips. Karen bends toward her. Is a poem coming?

Liz is premier, the first, the oldest, the kindest, the keeper of the peace. Liz Louise Freed. Presently a poet. A round, freckled face; a long, rounded body; long, round arms; long, round legs. Beautiful, round Liz. The freckles spread from her face to her neck, over her breasts to her waist. Then they end. She wears turtlenecks under her sweaters in winter and turns pale if you mention her freckles. One of Liz's poems:

> Half giraffe is she
> Behind the veil, blinks and blinks.
> Eye of the morning

3

Eye of the night, dark night.
Half queen is she
Her royal double progress
Unseen.

"It's the end I don't get," Tobi had said.
Liz only smiled. She won't explain her poems.
Years ago, though, they were easier to understand.
Karen still remembers a poem Liz wrote for one of
her birthdays.

Five is a funny age to be.
Five thinks it's smart.
Five thinks it's awfully wise.
Then you get to be six
And, whoops, you open your eyes!

So you're six, I say.
You're six today.
You're six, good cheer!
You're six, that's really fine.
You're six — want a glass of wine?

It was Liz who gave Karen a journal for her eighth
birthday, an oversized book, with a gray striped
cloth cover and thin red lines down each page. On
the cover, in big gold letters, .

The first thing Karen wrote: "Tobi and me to the
movies. She puts on eyeshadow in the ladies' room.
We buy M&Ms."

The next thing: "Today, saw a dead pigeon dead
in the road. A horrible sick sight."

And after that: "Liz is beautiful, kind, and nice.
I do love her freckles. Tobi to the movies with her

4

girl friend. I do hate her. She snores at night."

She decided to give her journal a name. Liz suggested Celeste. "It means heavenly. It's one of my favorite names."

Karen felt Celeste was one of her favorite names, too. "Dear Celeste, today Tobi says I run like a duck. I sock her once. She socks me three times." "Dear Celeste, spaghetti with disgusting clams again for supper." "Dear Celeste, Franklin Hocker comes up to me in the market and says ha ha boobs and looks at mine. What for, Tobi says, you don't have any."

After that, a long silence. Now and then, over the years she'd take the journal out of her desk, write in it for a few days, then forget it again. Liz was the writer in the family. Liz wrote in her journal every day. She had a desk drawer full of journals. No one went near that drawer on pain of death. No, not death. Tobi would kill you for doing something wrong. Liz would excommunicate you.

Since Liz had become a dedicated poet and quit her full-time job in an ad agency, she wore overalls instead of skirts, worked half-time in a bakery, and spent hours in her room writing.

"All that time alone is softening your brain," Tobi said. "Why do you speak so slowly? You sound like you're pulling taffy."

It was true, Liz's speech had slowed down like a faulty record. And not only that, sometimes they caught Liz watching them as if they were birds in the zoo.

"What are we, your raw material?" Tobi said. Liz didn't deny it.

Their father had wanted Liz to go to dental school,

follow in his footsteps. "I'm sorry, Dad," Liz said, sounding genuinely regretful. "Maybe if I don't make it as a poet?" Meanwhile she kept scraps of paper in her pockets and scribbled mysterious phrases with a tiny stub of pencil.

After Liz, came Tobi. If her sisters were desserts, Karen thought, Liz would be cool pineapple sherbet; Tobi would be dark bittersweet chocolate.

Tobi Rachel Freed. The story of Tobi's life: She wants what she wants when she wants it — and no waiting! Tobi's on the run, in every way. She's thin as a whip, runs four miles every morning before she goes to classes, works for the city directory, wants to do something significant with her life; her goal right now is to be a speech therapist. She broods that she's not doing enough with each day. "I sleep too much," she says, and sets her alarm clock for half an hour earlier.

She's not pretty the way Liz is, but there's something about her that makes people turn and look again. Karen has seen it happen. But don't try to tell Tobi that. "I'm so funny-looking. These teeth! You'd think Dad could do something." Tobi thinks her front teeth are too big, tries not to laugh, and when she does, covers her mouth. When Karen was a baby, Tobi bit her with those big teeth two or three times. She says now, when Karen brings it up, "How could I help myself? You looked so plump and juicy. Like a nice fat turkey leg." That hurts. Karen is always on the verge of dieting. "Besides," Tobi says, "I was probably hungry, was all. No mean intentions, dear sister."

Dear sister, indeed. How come Tobi sometimes

still looks at her that same way? When Tobi is mad at her, all Karen can see are Tobi's teeth, her big big white teeth.

And Karen, the third of the Freed girls. The last. Following behind Liz and Tobi through every grade in school, she was never just Karen Elizabeth Freed, but "Liz Freed's youngest sister" or "Tobi Freed's other sister." That's why Karen is greeted at the beginning of every semester with smiles and asked if she's going to keep up the Freed standards (probably not), if she's going to be half as good a student as Liz (don't think so), and if "we" have another candidate for track team, like Tobi? Karen's favorite teacher is always the new teacher who never knew either of her sisters.

Once — she must have been no more than seven — Liz woke her in the middle of the night. Tobi was there, too. "Get up," Tobi said. "Get dressed. Be quiet. Stop yawning. We're going someplace. Don't ask so many questions."

They tiptoed past their parents' room, Karen held her breath, her father snored. Tobi began to giggle, they ran down the stairs and out of the house, not quiet at all. "We're going to see the sun rise," Liz said. They jostled each other down the street, the air was sharp in their lungs. Liz led the way with the flashlight. On a muddy hill above the Catholic cemetery, Tobi knelt, turning to the east. A wind blew the last stars out.

Karen sneezed. "Shh!" Tobi said. "Kneel!" The sky clouded and a spatter of rain fell. Karen's knees hurt. The rain became serious. "Even though you don't see it," Tobi said, "the sun is rising and we are paying homage." She bent over, throwing out her arms. "Sun, sun, we honor you, sun." Liz snickered and Tobi was angry. "What's so funny, Miz Liz!" They went home, hair wet, knees muddy, and crowded into the bathroom together to pee and take showers.

TWO

There's a picture in the tin box where they keep their family snapshots. Liz, wearing shorts and a striped shirt, stands between Karen and Tobi, who are also wearing shorts and striped shirts. Their arms are linked, they are looking into the camera (probably held by their father) and each one of them is making a face. Liz's face, naturally, is the mildest; she's wrinkled up her nose, puffed out her lips. Tobi's face is the most frightening — her eyes are rolled up into her head and she's somehow managed to twist her features all out of shape. Karen, who's about seven, is sticking out her tongue and crossing her eyes, a talent she was proud of at that age. Since the picture is in black and white, it's not at first apparent that their striped shirts are exactly alike. Black and red stripes. Their Katoli shirts. Their Katoli faces.

Karen-Tobi-Liz, the Katoli, their three names knotted together. And what, Karen used to think, if they had called themselves The Litoka? Then she

9

would have been last again. As usual. As always!

Their slogan: The Katoli For Good or Evil. Good had been tremendously boring things like raking leaves or cleaning up a bathroom. Evil had been much better. Salt in the sugar bowl. Opening their parents' mail. Stealing quarters from the change jar in the kitchen. Knotting the living room curtains.

The Katoli didn't last nearly long enough for Karen. Around the time she was ten or so, things changed. There were her sisters, teenish and cool, and there was she, the fool kid. Still hoping her sisters would sleep in her room. Still waiting for them to have one of their satisfying fights over which one loved her the most. ("I do! . . . No, I do! . . . I took care of her when she was a baby! . . . Oh, I suppose it wasn't me who spent a whole summer wheeling her in her little stroller?")

Suddenly it was all gone. She plodded to school, telling herself she could live. She made a point of being jolly with her friends, but at home, her sisters made faces about her to each other and said, "What's the matter with Karen? She's sooo sensitive." Always getting upset over little things, they said. Trifles! Tiny nothings, like Liz and Tobi closing a door in her face ("No, Karen, you can't come in now") or whispering together ("Ka-ren, this conversation is not for you") or going out with each other to have a wonderful time without her. ("Look, you're just too young.")

It was in that period that she had a short career as an obsessive.

She ate nothing but cold cereal and canned beets for breakfast, said the word harmony as often as possible (as in, "Yes, my bed is made, be of good harmony"), counted every street light she passed, and wore only red socks and green sweaters.

Also, she dreamed hard enough about the family moving someplace else (a new start in life, a new Karen, her sisters enchanted and thus restored to her) to make it seem real. She considered Alaska, but settled on Mexico. She liked heat. Phase One was to give away things she didn't really need to take with her. She started by donating her Nancy Drews to a girl named Lori.

Lori was impressed. "I'll never forget you, Karen. Even if you live in Mexico forever. You're the most wonderful, generous person in the entire universe." Karen thought so, too, until talking to her mother one day, she said, "Mexico. . ." and her mother said, "Sweetie, Mexico? Where in the world — ?" She laughed. "I wouldn't mind, but we could never pry your father away from his practice."

That summer Liz was working, their mother taking courses at the college, and Karen and Tobi were home alone together. "Do everything I say," Tobi said, "and you can be my best friend." That seemed a small price to pay for best friendship with Tobi. It was almost as good as the Katoli. They baked butterscotch cookies, slept in the same room, made up plays, jumped rope, and played Monopoly, one continuous game, day after day, flat on their stomachs on the living room rug, the venetian blinds drawn against the sun. Staggering away, surfeited with money and deals, they would make a pot of fudge and eat it all at once, shushing each other's giggles. "Don't say a word to Dad. . . . Put the sugar away! . . . There, behind the ketchup! . . . Should we brush our teeth?"

11

One wet, hot night, three boys in a car crashed headlong into the enormous old oak in front of the Gitanos' house down the street from the Freeds. One boy died instantly, the other two, hours later. The morning paper ran front-page pictures of the crash, the boys, their weeping families.

In the middle of the night, Tobi got in bed with Karen. "You want to go someplace with me?" Karen was awake at once. "Where?" "Don't ask questions, it's special."

They dressed, crept down the stairs. Tobi had taken a wreath of flowers from her room. Karen had forgotten to put on shoes; outside the sidewalk was cool and gritty underfoot. They held hands, walked swiftly down the street, past the dark, sleeping houses. Where the car had smashed into the oak tree, there was a deep gash, a bloodless wound. Metal and glass were strewn all over the street and lawns.

Tobi bent over, put the flowers at the base of the tree, wiped her eyes. "Never tell." They ran back home in the swaying shadows of the trees, gulping air frantically.

Two days later, there was another story in the morning paper. Their mother read it out loud at breakfast. ". . . and no one on Morningale Avenue could tell this reporter who left the wreath of wild flowers at the tree where the lives of three young boys were so tragically cut off. Whoever it is also left a note tucked into the wreath. 'To Sandy, Amos, and Rick, rest in peace. Sandy, I'll never forget you as long as I live.' "

Tobi, pale and proud, fixed Karen with her eyes. Karen poured milk recklessly over the cornflakes;

the bowl overflowed. Her mother sighed at her carelessness. Later, Karen said, "Did you love him? Do you?"

"Never speak of it," Tobi said. "Never."

It was the end of the summer. One morning Tobi looked at Karen through the hair falling into her eyes. "Why am I wasting my time on you, child?" She rampaged through Karen's closet and bureau, grabbing armfuls of her stuff. On her way out, she banged into the shelf where Karen had her seashells arranged, and for good measure kicked the door. Later, she came back, shrugging, flipping books on the floor. She fell down on Karen's bed and looked meanly at her for a long time. Tobi had violet eyes and the worst sneer in the world. "Why do you write in that stupid diary, Karen? You have nothing to write about. Your life is silly and boring."

"Tobi —"

"Diaries are not for silly little people like you."

"Tobi! Anyway, it's a journal, not a diary."

"Journal? *Journal?* Talk English."

"That is English."

"My dear. That is pretentious English. Journal is a pretentious word for diary, my dear. Do you know whereof I speak? Do you understand the word *pretentious*, or should I put the message into simple language? Journal, little sister, is a stuck-up word for diary."

Tobi, Karen knew, could keep this up for hours. Bit by bit Karen felt herself falling into a pit, a black hole where she was disappearing. The scream started in her stomach.

When Liz came home, she pried them apart. "Really, Tobi. Why can't you two be friends?" Karen

13

saw how Liz's lumping Tobi with her enraged Tobi. Oh, well, good! She didn't care. She hated her fickle sister. She went off with Liz to her room to look through Liz's clothes and try on her earrings. But after a while, she was bored and went looking for Tobi.

That summer, too, Liz got her driver's license and Karen saw Paradise Lake for the first time. Both things on the same day. Or at least that's the way Karen remembers it — the two events connected forever in her mind.

The memory is this: Liz jubilantly waving the license, herself curled up on the window seat in the living room, watching Liz, her stomach aching with the thought that comes to her like a warning: Now Liz is a grown-up. At the instant of the thought, Liz seems to become at once larger and then, in a moment, dizzyingly smaller. Not smaller in the sense of little, but only as someone is smaller who is seen from a vast distance.

Immediately after, as if the two events happened in sequence, Karen's memory puts her in the back of the car, Liz and Tobi up front. Liz is driving, sitting up very straight, and Tobi is singing, off-key, of course. Karen is happy because she's with both of them and today they're all friends. She leans toward the front seat, leans between them, putting a hand on each of them, until Tobi complains that her hand is hot and sticky and pushes it away.

But Liz, never taking her eyes off the road, pats and squeezes Karen's hand, and suddenly Karen loves Liz so much she gets dizzy again and falls back into the seat where she rolls around and kisses the upholstery, announcing in a loud, silly voice, "I'm kissssing the caaaaar, guys."

And all the time they are driving through tunnels of green, and past wide fields, the sky is enormous and blue, and Karen is weak with pride in Liz, who jams on the brakes and sedately makes a turn. Dust billows up behind the car. Cows look over a wire fence. A man comes out of a little trailer and scratches his stomach.

Ahead of them, Karen sees a castle, a gleaming white castle with flags and turrets. Even though they are on a dusty road, it doesn't surprise her at all; it seems, in fact, completely right, and Karen knows that this is where her sisters are taking her, this is the destination, this castle with the sun blazing off the shining turrets.

The castle turns out to be a flag-draped arch with a big red-and-white sign, WELCOME TO PARADISE LAKE. Karen is a little disappointed that it's not a real castle, but all the same, it's wonderful. They pass through the arched entrance; there's a little booth with a woman inside. "Quarter each," she says.

"My sister drove us here," Karen says, her nose dripping with pride and excitement. Tobi pokes her, Liz puts down three quarters, and they clatter across the wooden decking and stand together, looking out at the lake.

Three

K aren was dancing. The cool morning air made
her drunk. She was Liz, round and golden
and beautiful with freckles. She was Tobi, small and
slender as a needle, violet eyes and a mouth that
could sneer or smile to kill you. She danced until
the sun broke through the window. She was Karen,
large and lumpish, big feet and knuckles on her
fingers she could crack like castanets.

She rode her bike to school, splashing through
every puddle. Later, she went home through Walnut
Park, looking for Tobi. The last few months Tobi
had taken up sketching. Where had that come from?
Did that have anything to do with speech therapy?
Tobi drew lumpish men on park benches, mis-
shapen trees, old women wearing strange hats. Karen
found her near the Civil War statue. Tobi was sitting
cross-legged on the grass, charcoal pencil in her
hand, sketch pad in her lap. She raised her eyebrows
in greeting and went on sketching.

Karen threw her bike down on the walkway and

took her camera out of her knapsack. She crouched on the grass, back against a tree, focusing on the feet passing through the lens. Boots . . . shoes . . . slippers . . . sneakers . . . and no two pairs of feet exactly the same. She shot rapidly, it was the only way; every photographer she'd ever read about said the same thing. Take the pictures, take ten, twenty, a hundred, maybe you'll get one good one out of the lot.

And as always she felt a fake. Did she really love photography? Did she burn with ambition? Was she talented? Or was it only her need to be one of the clever Freed sisters, to have her own niche? In her lens, a pair of red high-heeled shoes with straps clicked past. She could do an entire series of photos on shoes. Was that unique? Or had someone already done it? Hadn't someone, somewhere, already done everything?

Every month or so, at the Light Gallery, there was a new photo show. For Karen, always an occasion for despair, although afterward she would imagine herself the famous photographer, hers the framed pictures lining the white walls of the gallery. *About her work, Karen Freed is remarkably reticent. "My work speaks for itself." Ms. Freed did comment, however, that the inspiration for* Shoes, A Statement *arose from an afternoon in a park when she was struck by the notion of footwear expressing the whole of one's character and personality. Ms. Freed's brilliant work has been shown in galleries all over the country, and the well-known art collecters, Daniel and Bernice Delay Horace, have just acquired her —*

"What are you doing?" Tobi said. Karen turned

17

her camera on her sister for a moment; Tobi's face hung in the lens. She swatted Karen's arm away. "Is there film in that thing?"

"No."

"God, Karen."

Brakes screeched. Karen's stomach jumped. Karen Worrywart, they called her in the family. She worried about money, school, the future, car crashes. If any of them were late coming home, she went into the automatic worry mode. What would I do if anything happened to Mom, Liz? . . . But except for the time Tobi fell off the couch and broke her arm, they were all intact. Healthy as horses, their mother said.

Karen swung her camera. A boy came running along the path. She watched his feet through the camera. Brand new sneakers with purple lightning marks along the sides. She watched the sneakers run past, watched his hands dip down, watched them grasp the handlebars of her bike. She swung the camera up as he swung up her bike and continued running with it.

"That boy just stole your bike," Tobi said.

Karen dropped her camera, astonished that what she'd just seen in the lens was actually so. It had been like seeing a news event on tv, a fire, a storm, a riot. Even though you knew it was real somewhere for someone, it wasn't real for you. Except this time, it was. She ran after the boy. He looked over his shoulder, ran awkwardly with the bike. Karen thought, What a dummy! Why doesn't he get on it and ride away? At the park entrance, she caught up with him. "That's my bike!"

He was skinny; acne covered his cheeks like a tattoo. "What are you talking about?"

Karen grabbed the handlebars. She could hardly speak. "Bike! My bike!"

"You're crazy." He kicked the wheel. "This old beat-up thing — I'll sell it to you for three dollars." He kicked the wheel again.

"Hey, you!" Tobi yelled from behind them and Karen heard her drumming feet.

The boy raised his arm; Karen thought he was going to hit her in the face. She flinched; at that moment he could have had her bike, but he dropped it and walked away.

"This dumb bike," Tobi said on the way home and she kicked it the way the boy had. "Do you realize how long we've had this? It was Liz's first. You should have let him steal it."

But it was precisely because it had been Liz's and then Tobi's that Karen cared about it.

"We're ho-oo-ome," Karen yelled when they walked into the house and Liz came downstairs from her room, her hands in her pockets, a princess in overalls descending from the tower. In the kitchen, Liz took a bowl of cold macaroni from the refrigerator. Karen and Liz dug in. Tobi picked at the food, one macaroni at a time.

"Have some," Liz said. "Here. Eat, you skinny rabbit." She pushed the bowl toward Tobi.

"No, no, I'm not hungry."

Tobi told Liz about the bike thief. "Karen ran after him. You should have seen the monkey, Liz, scooting down the length of the park after that crudo." Tobi took another macaroni from Liz's plate.

"She was yelling. I mean screaming; no wonder he took off."

"Screaming? I don't remember that. *You* were screaming. I was screaming, too?" Karen stuffed in more macaroni to keep from smiling her pleasure.

Four

"D oes your father kick up a fuss that your mother works?" Marisa asked.

"What we say in our house," Karen said, "is that my father's money pays the mortgage and my mother's money puts the food on the table."

Marisa nodded. She had a face like a polished penny — round and gleaming. "I like that. My father won't hear of my mother working."

When Karen first met Marisa she was impressed by her hint of a foreign accent. Anything Marisa said — it could be as ordinary as "pass the salt" — sounded better because of that tiny exotic twang to her words.

Marisa's father was an executive with an international computer company and Marisa had lived a good part of her life in France, England, Germany, and Switzerland. She'd gone to at least eight different schools and along the way, Karen thought, besides her delicious accent, she had picked up a lot of poise, a lot of polish.

"Karen!" someone called. It was Liz, leaning out of Scott's pickup truck.

Marisa and Karen walked over. Scott's truck was bright red with his company's logo, a hammer and saw inside a circle, painted on the door. Underneath was the name, Hammar and Sawyer. Scott was the Sawyer part of the company. Guy Hammar was his partner. "It's just one of those funny coincidences," he'd explained when Liz first brought him home. "That our names are so perfect for the work we do."

"We're off to investigate a dog for Scott," Liz said. "Down Derider way. Want to come?"

"Want to?" Karen asked Marisa. They'd been planning on shopping.

"Oh, yes." Marisa looked so happy it made Karen feel a little guilty. Marisa was an only child. Every once in a while she would say, "Karen, come and eat supper with me tonight." It usually turned out that she'd been alone for the past three or four or five nights in their huge, formal house.

Marisa and Karen crowded into the truck. Karen sat next to the window, Marisa between her and Liz. They slung their knapsacks on the floor and put their feet on them. Karen liked the way Scott drove — a lot of concentration, but loose at the same time. The last time her mother gave her a driving lesson, she said Karen was so tense she was afraid she'd spasm her neck. No wonder. Karen had been worrying the whole time that she'd do something stupid and wreck them.

"Karen told me you wrote poetry, Liz." Marisa said *Lizss*, and Scott smiled at her.

"Well . . . I try."

"I'm in awe of poets," Marisa said. "I don't understand how they do it. Do you have a favorite poet, Liz?"

"My rival," Scott said. "She's always quoting him."

"Who?" Karen said. And then, remembering the poems tacked up to the bulletin board over Liz's desk, she said, "Donald Hall?"

"You see," Scott said. "Everybody knows. She even likes his name better than mine. She wants me to change my name to Donald."

Liz and Scott had been going together for almost a year. For the first six months or so, the family hardly saw him. Nothing new. Ever since she had been fourteen, Liz had had a string of boyfriends who came and went, not one lasting more than six months. Scott, Karen had heard her father say, was going for the distance. The whole nine yards.

Karen leaned against the window, watching Scott. Every year, downtown, there was a sidewalk art show. Hundreds of paintings, mostly of red barns and white birch trees and little kids with big eyes, but once, Karen remembered, she'd seen a painting of an angel descending to earth in a cloud of light. A real charmer of an angel with a mass of curly blond hair and eyes that were as warm and friendly as a little dog's. Scott's hair was dark, and instead of robes and wings he wore flannel work shirts and steel-tipped work boots, but otherwise he might almost have been the model for that darling, curly-haired angel.

"Dogs are one thing Scott and I disagree on, Marisa," Liz said. She put her arm across Scott's neck. "Don't get me wrong, I don't hate dogs. But I don't

23

exactly like them, either. Pant pant pant pant, do you love me, do you love me, do you love me? They're really insecure."

"You don't feel that way about dogs, do you, Karen?" Scott said.

She smiled, shook her head.

"You see," he said to Liz. "Karen likes dogs."

The dog was gone by the time they got to Derider. "I'm disappointed," Scott said to the woman who'd run the ad.

"Ohh," she said sadly. "You would have been good. You look like you love dogs." She wore bright red lipstick and a bright red sweater. "We were just heartbroken that we had to give up our little Shelley."

"Was he a nice dog?"

"The best. Wonderful personality. So bright and loving, just a real human being."

On the way home, they stopped for pizza. Marisa and Karen sat on one side of the booth, Liz and Scott on the other. "Well," Liz said, "I have to confess I feel a little sorry that Scott missed out on Shelley."

"You do?" Scott looked amazed.

"He might have been a special dog, less doggy than most dogs. I mean," she said, sucking up a piece of straying cheese, "considering who he was named after."

"Who's that?"

"You know, sweetie."

"I do?"

"Yes, I'm sure you do." She appealed to Marisa and Karen. "You two know, don't you? Hint," she said. " 'Nothing in the world is single, All things

by a law divine in one another's being mingle —
Why not I with thine?' "

"You wanted my being to mingle with a dog?"
Scott said.

"You're all a bunch of boors," Liz said. "Shelley.
Percy Bysshe Shelley!" At their blank looks, she
sighed. "The poet, the famous, wonderful, dead
poet."

"You think those people named their dog after
a poet?" Scott said.

"Yes."

"Come on, you know who they named the mutt
after. That fat actress — Shelley, Shelley what's-her-
name."

"It was a male dog," Liz said. "Why would they
name him after an actress?"

"Makes as much sense as naming it after a famous, wonderful, dead poet."

When Scott stopped at Marisa's house, Karen got
out of the truck first to let her out. "Scott's beautiful," Marisa whispered, putting her knapsack over
her shoulder. "I don't see how you keep from having
a violent crush on him."

"Oh, well . . . I don't."

Five

Rain lulled Karen to sleep that night, and then woke her in the morning. Above her, in the attic, she heard the steady *drip drip drip* of water into the pans. "We're going to float away," her mother said every time it rained, which meant that the leaks in the roof hadn't, by some longed-for miracle, repaired themselves.

"As long as they don't get worse," her father would say.

In the attic, Karen emptied pans out the window. On the street, cars swished by with their lights on. Two little kids in yellow raincoats passed. She imagined Scott's truck pulling up to the curb. He'd get out . . .walk up to the house. . . . She'd watch him until the last moment. Then she'd lean out the window. Scott! He'd look around, puzzled, then look up, see her and smile, his angel smile. And leap up, leap straight into the air and come flying through the attic window.

Shivering in her pajamas, Karen went downstairs.

Tobi's door was ajar and Tobi was awake, the covers pulled up to her chin. "Close the window," she said.

Karen got in bed with her. "Ohh, so warm in here."

"It was, until you arrived. Your feet are like ice." Tobi lay back, her head on her arm. "Look at that ceiling." The plaster was hanging like stalactites. "Any day now it's going to fall down and kill me. And you know what Dad'll do? Nothing."

"Well . . . he's not so handy around the house."

"A dentist not being handy is a contradiction in terms, Karen. The truth is Daddy doesn't care. He could live in a shack and so long as he had plenty of people to let him poke around in their mouths he'd be happy. This whole house is falling apart. Do you know how many years we've had those pans in the attic?"

"A long time."

"You bet!" Tobi pulled Karen's chin around. "I'll tell you something. . . . Can you keep a secret?" She took a snapshot out of her night table drawer and held it out to Karen. A large, bulky man sprawled on the steps of a house. He wore jeans, desert boots, a mocking smile beneath his brushy mustache. Beer can in hand, he saluted the camera.

Karen leaned up on her elbow. "Who is it?" she said. "I think he's bowlegged."

"Does it show?" Tobi studied the picture. "He's one of my instructors. A sculptor."

"You're taking sculpting? I thought you wanted to work with learning-disabled kids."

"It's a general art course. Anyway, don't be such a yahoo. I'm going to college to broaden myself."

27

"I haven't noticed you've gained any weight."

"That isn't even worth a snicker." Tobi took the snapshot back.

"Why do you have his picture?"

"I might bring him here sometime." She paused. "We're in love."

Karen fell back on the bed. Liz and Scott. Now Tobi and — "What's his name?"

"Jase. Jason. Jason Wade Wilson."

"Funny name," Karen sniffed. Tobi and Jason. Liz and Scott. And me? she thought. Karen and Davey? Was that love? Something, probably, but not love.

"Don't say anything to anyone." Tobi flopped over on her stomach. "Do I have a zit on my back?"

"Two," Karen said meanly.

"Two! Pick them."

There was something so satisfying and so disgusting about picking. She always wanted to. She always felt ashamed. And yet, the more disgusting it was and the more ashamed she felt, the more she wanted to laugh.

"Did you ever think," Tobi said, her voice muffled by her arms, "how in this family we have a little niche for everyone? Liz is the most beautiful and creative. I am the smartest and most passionate. Mom is the gutsiest and most practical. Dad is the most idealistic and dreamy. We all pretend to be humble and modest, but don't we really judge everyone else by how they measure up to the fabulous Freeds?"

"You forgot me," Karen said.

"Oh, God." Tobi turned over. "Let me see, where do you fit into the family mythology? You,

Karen —" She looked blank for a moment. "Well, you — you're our monkey."

"No, that's disgusting."

"Oh, well, then, you're —" Again Tobi paused. "Okay, you're — *you.*" She rolled out of bed. "Don't you have to get ready for school? I'm going to take a shower."

You're you. Was that it? The whole thing? That remark of Tobi's rankled. Karen couldn't forget it, but cowardly her, she didn't say anything. She had once read a story that began, "Cowards are the nicest people." Maybe so. She didn't think acting like a coward made her nice. What it made her was mad at herself.

For a couple of days she kept going back to that moment in her mind, thinking of all the things she should have said. *Look, Tobi, you gave everybody else a character. What am I, to you, a cipher? A zero? A zit?*

Finally she said it, caught Tobi in the upstairs hall. "Tobi, you said something on Tuesday I want you to explain."

Tobi looked at her incredulously. "You want me to remember what I said a week ago?"

"Two days ago," Karen said. "Tuesday morning. We were in your room. We were in bed and you showed me what's-his-name's picture, that art teacher —"

"Shh!" Tobi grabbed her arm. Considering how thin she was, it was amazing how hard Tobi could grab. She had a lot of muscle. "I told you not to say anything about him."

Karen shook her hand off. "Will you listen? You were talking about us, our family. And you said

29

that in our family Liz was the creative one and Mom was this and Dad was that —"

"Okay, okay, I'm always talking that way, so what?"

"And then, Tobi, you said about me. 'And you, Karen, you're you.' "

"So? Well?"

"So! Well! Well, this, Tobi. What does that mean? 'You're you.' You can't think of anything else to say about me?"

"God, Karen! What's the big fuss? I don't get this. How do I know what I meant on Tuesday morning? Probably nothing. It was just a remark. Look, why don't you relax and take it as it comes?" She went into her room. "Don't be so sensitive," she added over her shoulder.

How many times had Karen heard that one? They were always saying it to her. Don't be so sensitive. You're so sensitive. Why are you so sensitive? "Tobi!" she shouted. "I am not sensitive!"

Tobi looked up from her desk, an expression of saintly patience on her face. "Gimme a break. I've got a paper to do for my psych course."

"Excellent!" Karen stamped down the hall to her room, slammed the door. Here she was fifteen, finally, more than half grown up, and here was Tobi accusing her — again! — of being too sensitive. It was an accusation, wasn't it? It meant she was still that same kid Karen, the little one, the little sister who was too easily upset over this and that, over little fol-de-rols that any mature and well-balanced person would take in stride. A fool, after all.

Six

W hat are you doing?" Karen said to David.
"Obvious, isn't it?"
"Too true. You're wrecking your mother's scale."
"Please. I'm fixing it." David held the scale to his
chest, grunting as he twisted the marker. He was
big — tall and big-boned — maybe a little fat around
the tummy, with a mop of black hair that was always falling in his face. "This thing has been set at
two pounds and two ounces for the last thousand
years. What's the point of having a scale if it's not
precise?"
"Oh, precisely." Karen found an opened can of
pineapple juice in the refrigerator. "You want some
juice?"
"Not now. Food interferes with my concentration."
"Nothing interferes with your concentration,
David." She sat down at the table, placing her goldfish in the plastic carrying bag next to the glass of
juice.

31

David and his mom lived in a little apartment over a grocery store. Karen liked being there; everything was small and cozy and neat.

She first knew Davey in elementary school when the Kurshes lived down the block on Morningale. That made her and Davey neighbors, but not exactly friends. She was willing, he wasn't. He palled around with four or five other boys. They played war games and had a secret club in a tree house where they had nailed up a huge sign: NO GIRLS ALLOWED.

When the Kurshes sold their house and moved away, Karen didn't miss David; she hardly gave him another thought.

In eighth grade, they met again. "Aren't you Karen Freed?" he said, coming up to her during a break in gym.

She saw a big boy with a mop of bushy hair, wearing a T-shirt that said, No Nukes Is Good Nukes. "Davey Kursh?"

"David, please."

"Sure, Davey."

He looked pained. "I mean it, Karen. I prefer David."

"Rightey-o, Davey."

He rolled his eyes up into his head. "Why do you hate me?"

"Just a little never-too-late revenge for the sign on your tree house."

"What sign?"

Coach blew the whistle and they separated. They were on opposing volleyball teams. "What sign?" he yelled, punching the ball her way.

All that week he'd come up to her in the halls

and say, "What sign? What sign? I don't remember any sign."

Finally, she said, "I'll give you a hint. Still hate girls?"

In answer, he gave her a big smile.

"You really don't remember that sign?"

He raised his hand. "I swear. Total blankout. You're going to have to tell me, Karen."

She had to admit he'd had a change of heart. The boy who wore a No Nukes T-shirt was not the boy who'd played war games. And he definitely didn't hate girls. That year, a lot of kids were giving parties and pairing off. Davey and Karen started getting invited as a couple. It was easy being with him, so without their ever actually deciding to go together, it happened. They became David-and-Karen.

After a while, he told her about his father, who had a rare disease of the nervous system. When Mr. Kursh first found out what his trouble was — that was when they lived down the block from the Freeds — he was able to work out of his house. He was an accountant, so he didn't really need to go to an office. "He got worse, sicker," David said. "And everything cost tons of money — doctors, tests, therapy, all that stuff." He shrugged. "We couldn't afford to live over there on Morningale anymore, so we moved. My father's in the Vet's Hospital now."

"When do you see him?"

"Weekends."

"That's really rough, David."

"Yeah. It is." His eyes got red.

After that conversation she felt close to him. He

came over to the house a few times, ate with the family. "Cute boy," Tobi said.

"Agreed," Liz said, "but not old enough to be really interesting."

"Oh," Karen said.

"Still," Tobi said. "Old enough for Karen."

Stand-up comedy, with her as the straight woman.

"David," she said now, "do you realize we've been going around together for almost two years?"

"Looooong time." He twisted harder and the scale pinged ominously.

"David. I want to ask you something. What kind of person do you think I am?"

"You're okay."

"Many thanks."

"Well, what do you want me to say?"

"It isn't what I want you to say, Davey. The point is, what do you want to say?"

"You're okay."

"Thanks, oh thanks. You, too."

She wandered into the living room. There was a dry cleaning store across the street, a car wash, a pizza place. A man passed on a three-wheel bike. He stopped at a trash can, picked out two empty soda bottles, stashed them into a wire basket with other empties.

In the kitchen David was still working away at the scale. She said, "You're not afraid of breaking it?"

"Have some faith, will you, Karen?"

"David, not to be mean about it, but you always break things. Remember that clock you were going to fix —"

"It was beyond repair, Karen. Nobody could have fixed it."

"— and your mother's toaster which, you told me, she ended up throwing out —"

"That is not very friendly to remind me of that."

"— and that little tv —"

"It was an old piece of junk. I thought I could resurrect it as a gift to my father."

"Your intentions are good. Where's Eggbert? You didn't break him, did you?"

David looked at her over the scale. "Eggbert?"

"Disaster! You've forgotten already?"

They were both doing the Health and Family Life unit this quarter. In the interests of teaching his class "what it means to be responsible for another soul," Mr. Albright had assigned each student the task of carrying around either an uncooked egg or a goldfish for two weeks. "Just think of that egg as your child. I want to see your child in school with you. If you want to leave your child, you have to get a baby-sitter. When you sit down to eat lunch, you must know where your child is and, in the case of those who choose a goldfish, you better make sure your child gets to eat properly."

"The egg," Karen said. "Eggbert. Your favorite kid, Davey. The friend of my kid, Gladys Goldfish."

"Karen, you're worrying a lot today." He pointed to the cupboard where Eggbert was sitting next to a heap of dirty dishes.

"Don't leave poor Eggbert there. He might get broken."

David sighed. "Say break or broken once more, go ahead, I dare you."

35

"Break. Broken. Brokest." She leaped up as he dived for her.

"You're not going to get away with this, Freed."

"Don't break anything," she yelled as they galloped around the furniture. He caught her in the corner between the couch and the tv. "Ah . . . uh . . . oh . . . David. Davey! You're breaking my ribs."

He didn't want to let go. Hugs and hands. And he was a lot stronger than she, although she didn't just limply let him do anything he wanted. Which, lately, was more and more. "Sex is natural," he'd informed her. "Haven't you heard the news? It's wrong to stifle your basic biology."

She hadn't known what to say to him. She'd talked to Liz about it, not quite coming out with it, picking her way delicately around the subject, as if it were a bomb that might go off in her face. But Liz knew. "Look, Karen," she said, "don't let him talk you into anything. I tell you that from personal experience. From where I am now, I can see I picked the wrong person and the wrong time. It was — not good. But even if it had been the right person and the right time — no, I don't think fifteen is exactly the right time for anyone. So think about it, Karen."

She had. She did. And she had come to some conclusions. "I love you a lot as a friend," she said now, holding Davey's hands.

"That's great. I love you a lot, too."

"But . . . ah . . . don't take this wrong; there's something missing."

"Hey, hold it! I'm all here. Nothing missing. Look."

"Quit that, Davey. I don't mean missing in you."

"You've got something wrong with you?"

"Maybe so." A disturbing thought. "Something's

missing in my feelings — do you know what I mean?"

He puffed up his lips, shook his head clownishly. "What is this missing mysterious matter?"

"I don't know," she said, "because I've never had it."

"Then maybe whatever is missing is not, in fact, missing. Maybe everything is where it's supposed to be. Me, boy. You, girl."

Karen smiled automatically. Davey was making a joke of it, but she was sure, she was absolutely positive that something was missing between them, some chemistry — yes, some mysterious matter. And if it weren't missing, if it were there, then she would know it and recognize it.

Seven

Sunday morning, Karen's mother was frazzled, at least as frazzled as she ever got which, on a scale of ten, was about a four. "Your grandmother's coming over," she announced, lighting a cigarette.

"Yeah, Ma, it's Sunday."

"Well, what are we going to feed her?"

"You say that every Sunday."

"Every Sunday it's a problem."

"Food will do fine," Karen's father said.

"Is that a dentist joke, Arnie? I was thinking meatballs, or —" She looked in the freezer. "I could heat up that casserole?"

"Meatballs," Karen said. "Garlic bread, salad."

"Good." Her mother's relief didn't last long. "This house is a mess. I didn't have a chance to do a thing all week. You're not going out, are you?"

"The house looks okay to me," Karen said.

"Librarians are cleaner," her mother said. A librarian joke.

The minute they heard housecleaning, Liz and

38

Tobi both disappeared. "I promised Scott. . . ." Liz jiggled her car keys.

And Tobi, in gray sweats and a white headband, said, "I'll join the fun when I get back," and jogged out the front door.

Karen felt surly at not being able to pull her own disappearing act. The phone rang. She took it in the kitchen. Maybe it was Marisa with some wonderful plan to rescue her from being the household drudge. "Hello."

"Dr. Freed?" a male voice asked. Yes, you idiot, sure, this is Dr. Freed. "Dad," she called. He picked up the phone upstairs.

"Arnie Freed speaking."

"Dr. Freed? Dr. Freed, I have a terrible toothache."

"How bad is it?"

"I didn't sleep all night."

Karen hung up. She knew the rest of the conversation. Did you try aspirin? Yes, Doctor. It didn't help? No, Doctor. Well, if you feel that bad, why don't you meet me in the office in half an hour?

Her mother said that her father had to be the only dentist in the United States without an answering service. No buffer. Nothing standing between him and his patients. They bleated and he ran. Karen couldn't imagine being that devoted to puffy gums, putrid mouths, and rotting teeth.

While her mother washed the kitchen floor, Karen sorted through the pile of stuff in the front hall. The closet there was a catchall for everybody's everything. "What a mess," Karen complained, walking through the kitchen with an armload of jackets to hang up in the back entryway.

"It's no more fun for me than for you." Her mother was bent over the mop, wringing it out in a bucket.

"At least you're used to it."

"What makes you think that?"

"It's your job, isn't it?"

"I thought being a librarian was my job. Or do you believe in sex-associated cleaning genes?"

"Well, I never see Dad do this."

"That's because he has office hours," her mother said, sitting back on her heels and lighting another cigarette. She puffed away, frowning. "I think that's the excuse, anyway."

When they were finally done, Karen took a couple of creamsicles from the freezer. She licked the frozen orange coat. "Reward food, Mom, don't make faces like that."

"Sweet stuff. Ruins your appetite."

"You'd like it, too, if you didn't smoke."

Once, Karen had gone across town to visit her mother at work. Ebbert Mingus Junior High. "Where's the library?" A kid pointed indifferently. Karen went up worn stairs, down a wide, green-walled corridor. A display case with book jackets, a sign on the door. COME IN AND DON'T BE QUIET. The library was buzzing, kids all over the place. Her mother stood with her arms crossed, listening to a small, dark boy in a striped T-shirt. She wore a full skirt, a red silk blouse, earrings, stockings. She seemed to be somebody Karen didn't know. Her mother put her hand on the boy's shoulder; they walked over to a bookshelf. Three girls hurried up to her. "Mrs. Freed! Mrs. Freed, you gotta help us.

40

We're desperate." They like her, Karen thought. For some reason it was shocking.

She wandered into her mother's study, a small, narrow room off the kitchen. The desk was snowed under with books and papers. This was where her mother did science book reviews for some magazine that only other librarians read. Karen could read the reviews only after they were published. Her mother's other writing was off limits because it was unpublished. She had written a story for little kids, "Don't Stop That Music," that she kept sending around to publishers and getting back in the mail.

Karen peeled the paper off the second creamsicle. Once her mother had said to her, "You know what my life wishes are for you, darling? That you find somebody good to share your life with and that you have work that you love. Then you'll be one of the lucky ones."

"Like you?" Karen had said.

Her mother had hesitated, then nodded. "Like me."

Karen remembered that hesitation. Sometimes she heard her parents fighting behind their closed bedroom door. Then she wondered about the things she and her sisters said about their parents. That they loved each other so exclusively, that they were neurotically dependent on each other. It was exciting to talk that way, but was it true?

"I wonder where Tobi is," her mother said, sitting down at the desk. "She couldn't be jogging all this time?"

At once, Karen imagined Tobi with the man in the photo, jogging by the reservoir, side by side, his

41

bow legs churning, Tobi's heels kicking up. She saw this so vividly. She said, "Yes. She is!"

The hall door slammed. "Tobi?" her mother called.

"Me," Liz answered. "Want some help?" she said, looking in. Scott hovered behind Liz. Over her shoulder, he waved to Karen.

Karen dropped the creamsicle sticks into the wastebasket, swiped at her mouth. Was she smeared orange? She hunched over to hide her stained sweat shirt.

"Your timing is great," her mother said to Liz. "Karen and I did it all. But if you want to sign up for next week —"

Liz was rosy; all her freckles stood out, the way they did when she'd just come out of the shower. "We took a ride," she said. "It's beautiful out."

"We went to see the house I'm working on," Scott said.

"The one Scott designed," Liz said.

"No, no, no. Don't give your mother the wrong idea. I did the drawings, but it's nothing complicated. I'm no architect."

"You could be," Liz said.

Scott looked from Liz to Karen to her mother, the same tender glance all around. "Listen to her," he said, putting his chin on Liz's head. They went out again, their arms around each other, and Karen and her mother heard Scott saying, "Come on, give me a little kiss!"

"There," Karen's mother murmured, "is a man who likes women."

Eight

M om?" Tobi said, coming into the kitchen, and bumped into Karen, as if she didn't see her standing right there with a handful of silverware. Was Tobi nervous? "I want you to meet someone, Mom," she said, and there he was, the man from the photograph, towering over Tobi, big and burly in a flannel shirt.

"This is Jason." Black eyes, a brushy, flowing mustache, and thick, black hair, long hair, down to his shoulders. And — aha, Karen had been right, bow legs.

"Pleased to meet you, Tobi's mom." He should have had a deep, resonating voice to go with the rest of him; instead it was light, smooth, almost a boy's voice. "I'd like to call you something else — and, really, not Mrs. Freed."

"Well . . . the name is Sylvia."

"I'm Karen." Not that anybody asked. Jason looked at her, looked down at her. Then his hand, a real bear paw, outstretched; a brief touch, and he returned the full force of his eyes to her mother. Ah, so. For him, she didn't count.

"Jason teaches at the college," Tobi said. "But we met jogging."

"At the reservoir," Karen said, remembering her "vision."

"What?" Tobi looked at her, frowning.

"You were jogging at the reservoir."

"You just met today?" her mother said.

They were all talking at once. From above them, Jason laughed. "No," Tobi said, "we didn't just meet today. Where'd you get that idea?" They'd known each other quite a while, she said. "I'm in one of Jason's classes." But they only got to talking as people, not teacher-student, one day when they were both jogging. "Around the rose gardens," she said. There went Karen's vision.

"So I guess it's, oh, two months now we've been seeing each other."

"Really," her mother said. "Two months?" She didn't like that. "That's a long time, Tobi . . ." Her voice trailed off. Fill in the end of the sentence. *. . . a long time for you to be seeing someone without your family knowing about it.*

"Mmm," Tobi said, sitting down and peeling an orange.

"How long have you been teaching, Jason?" her mother asked.

"Ten years, Sylvia."

"Ah. And is that all you've ever done?"

She was fishing, wanting to know how old he was. Karen wondered the same thing. He looked nearly as old as her father; his neck was brown and crinkled.

Jason put a cigarette between his lips — the original Marlboro man. "Mind if I smoke?" Surprise! That light boy voice again.

Tobi got up, threw the orange peel into the garbage. "Mom's a smokestack, herself."

"Before I taught, Sylvia, I bummed around a bit, worked as a gandy dancer on the railroads, picked up work here and there, enough to keep going as an artist, enough to keep my family together."

"Family?" her mother said.

"Jason's staying for dinner," Tobi said. "Okay?" She leaned against him, a taut stick leaning against a tree, and in her eyes, in her glance upward, there was something that turned their mother's nose faintly blue at the wings.

Karen's father came into the kitchen then, and he and Jason shook hands. "Jason Wade Wilson, sculptor," Jason said and, without missing a beat, he added, "Remember that name. It's going to be famous."

"Arnie Freed," her father said, and passed his hand over the bald spot on the back of his head. His mode was modesty.

Then there was a lull in the conversation, one of those dead spots when nobody knows what to say. In fact, Karen thought, Jason was the only one who looked at ease. He stamped out his cigarette butt in the sink, brought out a rumpled pack, and lit another cigarette.

"Would you like to see the backyard?" her father said finally.

"Sounds good to me." The two of them went out.

Karen's mother turned to Tobi. "How old is he?"

"Thirty-five." Tobi stuck her chin out.

45

Karen did a bit of elementary math. Seventeen years older than Tobi. Ten years younger than her father, only eight years younger than her mother. And if you got right down to it, old enough to be her, Karen's, father.

Her mother must have been doing the same math. "He's too old for you. He could almost be your father! What is he doing with a green, eighteen-year-old girl?"

"Green!" Tobi's voice rose. "Thanks, oh thanks. For your information, we're in love."

Her mother's nose turned blue again, then white. "Tobi —"

"Age doesn't matter." Tobi cut her off. "I don't care. He doesn't care. Why do you care?"

"He's had other relationships," her mother said.

"So?"

They were talking over each other.

"What was that about a family?"

Tobi hesitated, then said defiantly, "He was married before."

Her mother stood in the middle of the kitchen, holding a stirring spoon, looking as if she wanted to clobber Tobi with it.

"And you might as well know, he has two kids."

"Wonderful."

"A boy and a girl. They live with their mother in Spain. She — Lara — went there a few years ago. It's awful for him, he never gets to see his kids and he misses them a lot."

"Then why doesn't he go live there?"

Their voices notched up another decible.

"Tobi, you're getting in over your head."

"It's my life."

"You're not even nineteen —"

"I told you! My age has nothing to do with it."

Stop it, Karen said. Stop. It. She thought she said it. Maybe she just imagined saying it. Her mother at the table, her hand over her mouth. Tobi leaning against the refrigerator, face glowing with anger and tears.

And just then they heard her grandmother calling, "Sylvia? Arnold? I'm here."

"So there you are," her grandmother said, as Karen came into the front hall. She was waiting by the staircase to be received. A real lady.

"How are you, Grandma?" Karen kissed her soft, bristly cheek.

"Are you working hard in school?"

"Yes, Grandma."

"You have to work, Karen. You can't be lazy."

"Yes, Grandma."

Her grandmother straightened her hat, a classy-looking felt fedora with a wide brim and a dark band.

Mrs. Freed, or Hattie, as she prefers to be called, is never seen anywhere, anyplace, anytime, without a hat. Quote unquote a newspaper article, written about twenty years ago and now hanging, framed, in her grandmother's living room.

One way or another, she had been making hats since she was a girl. *"I used to make hats out of nothing, a bit of ribbon and a little scrap of material. I went to work as a milliner when I was fifteen; I had to help out my family."* Later, she had become a hat designer for a big manufacturer. And much later still, she had opened her own shop, Creations

47

by Hattie. *"A dream come true,"* she had told the reporter.

Now, with the fedora, she wore a draped midnight blue dress, a string of blue glass beads, and matching blue stone earrings. She had a big, deep voice and big, fat, strong arms. An impressive woman. Even her earlobes were impressive, large and thick, fleshy as thumbs.

"Too bad none of you take after your father," she said. Grandma's lament. "Arnold was an exceptional student. Do you know that he went to medical school when he was only nineteen?"

"Yes, Grandma."

"Brilliant. A brilliant boy. He could have been a surgeon. Of course you three girls are bright enough," she said, sounding regretful at having to concede so much. Tobi had once said that if their father had been able to conceive and give birth to the three of them on his own, a holy male birth, without their mother's taint, their grandmother would think they were brilliant, too.

Karen followed her grandmother into the living room, brought her the fruit tray, showed her the new issue of the school paper. She had a photo in it of a blue jay sitting on a roof of a house next to a tv antenna. "Very nice," her grandmother said. Karen winced. Why had she trotted the paper out? When she developed the photo she had thought it inspired, a satiric comment on modern life. Now it seemed banal, even pointless.

Her grandmother sat upright in the chair, her eyes bright, looking around to see if anything had changed since the previous Sunday. "I'm seventy-six," she liked to tell people. "I look much younger. People are amazed when they hear my age."

Karen's mother came in. "Mother Freed, hello." She kissed the older woman. "Dinner's almost ready." Then everyone else appeared. Tobi kissed her grandmother. Liz was there and stepped up. "How are you, Grandma?" She hugged her and Grandma patted Liz's face. Everyone got in line, even Scott. Jason smiled under his mustache. Hang around a while, Karen thought, you'll be kissing her, too.

Grandma beckoned to Jason. "A teacher? At the college?"

"Teaching's a sideline," Jason said. "Cruel necessity. I'm an artist."

Grandma pursed her lips fastidiously. "I don't suppose you make a living at that, either." Why did everything she say sound like God's word to Moses on the mountain?

"I do all right. I don't think about it any more than I have to."

Karen watched the two of them dueling. Worthy opponents. She enjoyed the contest — this was different than Tobi and Mom going at each other.

"Food, folks." Karen's father set a bowl down in the middle of the table.

"Arnold," her grandmother said, "sit down, dear, you look tired. Are you overdoing things?"

"I'm fine, Ma."

"Then you must be getting old."

"It happens to us all," her father said mildly.

"Does it?" Grandma sat up even straighter.

Liz tapped her spoon on her glass. "Hello, everybody, I have something to tell you all." She held out her hand. Among her silver rings was a new one on her thumb. "Scott and I are now engaged to be engaged."

A hum of talk arose. "Engaged to be engaged," her grandmother said. "What kind of nonsense is that?"

Karen's father tipped back in his chair. "That's a new one on me, too, Mother."

"Congratulations," Karen's mother said, and added, "I think."

"Come on, guys." Tobi raised her eyebrows at Liz. "You people act like you're in the Stone Age. You've heard of that. Everyone does it."

Karen toyed with her melon. So Liz and Scott were making their relationship really tight. Scott was going the distance, all right. She might even have a brother-in-law sometime soon. So why didn't she feel terrific and happy?

"You have two children?" her grandmother was saying to Jason.

"Right. My daughter's name is Georgia. Named after Georgia O'Keefe."

"The artist," her grandmother said.

"My son's named after Picasso."

"How very interesting."

"When he lived here, Pablo was a funny name, but in Spain, it's ordinary as dirt. So I'm told by my wife. The bitch."

The word dropped into the conversation like a stone in water. A short, vibrant pause. Tapping the edge of her glasses on her mouth, Karen's mother looked at Jason. And Tobi, her face flashing warning signals, looked at her mother. You could always tell when Tobi was on the verge of exploding. She got red right under the roots of her hair.

Karen's stomach clenched. She pushed back her chair and left the table. "Where are you going?" her mother said.

"My camera," she improvised hurriedly.

She stood in the doorway, snapping pictures, focusing on hands. Grandma's hands, liver-spotted, strong. Her father's hands, the blunt, clean nails. Scott's, bitten-down, raggedy nails, a blood blister on one of his fingers.

"Take me and Scott," Liz said.

Karen took deep breaths, unclenching her stomach. The dangerous moment seemed to have passed. Jason was devoting himself to the food. Her mother had put her glasses back on. Karen stood up on a chair, focused. Liz and Scott. Tobi and Jason. Mom and Dad. Click . . . click . . . click. . . . All those pairs. This was a regular Valentine. To rumple things up a little, she took Mom and Grandma, Scott and her father, Jason and Liz. Uncouples. A series. The happy family at the table. Sweet Harmony in Suburbia. *Ms. Freed is know for her satiric yet sympathetic exposition of suburban life. . . .*

"Too bad you didn't invite David over today," Liz said when Karen sat down again.

"How is the boy?" Tobi, though, was still perched on the edge of her chair, as usual picking at her food. "Is he still going to be the brilliant young scientist?"

"I guess."

"And who," said Grandma "is David?"

"My friend."

"Friend? Do you mean you have a boyfriend, Karen? You're too young for a boyfriend, darling."

51

Karen's father zeroed in for a wink. Liz smiled, tapped her lips. Another poem coming? At once, Karen remembered a funny, slightly humiliating moment some weeks ago. Rashly, she had said to Liz, "Why don't you write a poem about me?"

And Liz, smiling, had obliged on the instant. "My sister Karen, she is so sweet. My sister Karen, she has cold feet. There's a poem, there's a poem about you. Is one enough? I can't do two." Karen's head flamed; she felt the injustice of being the youngest in this family. When would they stop treating her like a joke?

"Are those all your own teeth?" Karen's father was saying. He leaned interestedly toward Jason. Had he really said that? Were all families as bizarre as hers?

She looked across the table, met Scott's eyes. He didn't smile, wink, blink, or look away, but watched her gravely. Something passed between them, some link, some unspoken message, and then he nodded, a tiny salute — only she saw it — as if he were telling her he understood. Understood what? Everything, she thought, everything.

Nine

T he more I think about it, Tobi," Karen's mother said, the next morning in the kitchen, "the more I know I just am not terribly thrilled with what'sisface."

"Jason. His name is Jason." Tobi's voice was like wire.

"Right. Jason. No, not thrilled with him, not thrilled at all." Her mother pulled a pack of cigarettes out of her skirt pocket.

"And I'm not real thrilled with your smoking," Tobi said. She stood in the doorway, nibbling half an orange, wearing her knapsack, looking over her shoulder. All ready for a quick get-away.

"That's a strange comparison." Their father was sitting in the dinette eating eggs and reading. Karen, across from him, glanced up in surprise. Who could tell that he was even listening? Usually, he left these family things up to her mother.

Her mother coughed, lit up. "And, by the way, Tobi, is that all you're having for breakfast?"

Tobi put down the orange. "Are we talking about food or my friends?"

"Anything you want."

"I don't want to talk about either one."

Karen hunched over her bowl of cornflakes.

"Just tell me this, Tobi," her mother said. "How serious is this thing with, er —"

"Jason. Jason. Jason."

"Right. Jason. He's going to be famous."

"That's right," Tobi flashed. "Then you won't be asking me how serious this thing is."

Bam. Bam. Bam. Karen pushed aside the bowl of soggy cornflakes. Shut up. I hate you both. Shut up.

"Well, Tobi has been through things before," her father said, sticking his finger in his book. "Remember when you took up the clarinet, Tobes?"

"The clarinet!"

"And dance. For a while you wanted to be a dancer."

"I did not!"

"I mean," he said mildly, "you have enthusiasms and perhaps —"

"I know what you mean!" Tobi ate arguments the way she wouldn't eat a piece of meat, getting it between her teeth, biting and chewing. "You mean Jason is one of Tobi's little enthusiasms. Here today, gone tomorrow. About as important as the clarinet. Well, think what you want, both of you!"

Karen and Tobi left the house together. "Are you on their side, too?" Tobi said. She didn't wait for Karen's loyalty oath. "I knew they'd have a cow about Jason. I told him. I told him they'd go crazy.

You know what he said? They're going to be crazy about me." She smiled proudly.

Lunch period, Karen ran into Davey on her way out of school. "Where're you going?" he asked. He looked handsome in a green shirt.

"Taking some film to be developed. Want to come along?"

"I don't have anything better to do."

"Don't get carried away with enthusiasm, Davey."

"David," he warned.

Outside, it was another warm, rainy, end-of-March day. Technically, they weren't supposed to leave the building during lunch break, but nobody ever said anything if you got back on time. David slung his arm over her shoulder. "Karen. Why don't we trot over to my house for a while?"

"Davey — David," she corrected herself, "you know we'll never get back on time if we start that."

"What?" he said innocently. "Start what? Maybe what I want to do is watch a little tv."

"Oh, right, you're a terrific soap opera fan."

"I can't convince you?" He let his hand drop lower.

Karen linked her fingers with his. "Does that shirt make you feel sexy?"

"Everything makes me feel sexy," he said seriously.

"Me?"

"Well, yes!"

Later, after school, she had an appointment with Rachel, the hygienist, in her father's office. The last time Karen had been into the office, the hygienist was Jenny; the time before that, Terri. It seemed as

55

if every time her father hired a DH, she immediately got married, moved west, or went back to school. And every time Terri-Rachel-Suzie-Mary-Pat-or-Jamie left him, her father would say, "Sometimes I think I have bad breath." Another dentist joke.

Into the chair, on with the baby bib, open the mouth. She turned her thoughts to Davey to keep them off the cleaning and scraping. What a coward! It wasn't true, as some people thought, that being the daughter of a dentist took away the fear and loathing. Her father had her on a six-month schedule, but Karen always canceled her appointment and made a new one. Putting off the dread day.

"You haven't been flossing too well, Karen."

"Mrrmrghh." About Davey now. She liked that she made him feel sexy. She liked feeling sexy, herself. The problem was — different definitions of sexy.

Rachel bent her spotted face over Karen. "Don't forget, brush gently, you don't want to injure your gums."

"Mrrmrghhh." The way it was with Davey, she felt constantly as if she were walking a tightrope. Teetering along a wire strung over a gorge —

Her father came in. "How's daughter number three doing?"

"I think she has some work over here, Dr. Freed."

Now they were both peering into her mouth.

— a gorge, and down below — crocodiles, rocks, a raging —

"You haven't been here in, let me see —" Rachel looked at the chart.

— furious river. If she leaned too far in either direction, slipped off that wire, it would be goodbye, Karen.

56

"It's over eight months, Karen," Rachel said.

Good-bye, Karen? No more Davey? Her breath caught in her chest. "Eight months?" she said, sitting up in the chair. "I wonder how that happened."

That evening she and Tobi were playing chess, the board between them on Tobi's bed. "Tobi," she said, "I want to ask you something."

"Shoot."

"It's about sex."

Tobi looked up from the board. "No."

"I didn't even ask you the question and you've got an answer."

Tobi leaned back on her hands. She was wearing a Jane Fonda leotard, purple and white stripes, gold belt, the legs cut way up on her thighs. "What do you want to know?"

"It has to do with Davey and me. I don't want specific advice so much as, ah, just, ah, a general —"

"If no won't do, Karen, spit it out."

She picked up a pawn and put it back down again. "Tobi, when did you first do it?"

"Hold it, hold it. What's that got to do with you and Davey?"

"Well, he's, ah —"

"Oh . . . so that's it."

"Right. We haven't exactly talked about it in so many words, but —"

"No," Tobi said again. "Don't."

One thing about Tobi, all her opinions were firm. Yes. No. Do. Don't.

"Why not?"

"You've got time."

"My idea is, I should be in love."

"Good, Karen. You just wait."

"Did you?"

"That's right."

"How old were you?"

"Karen —" Tobi leaned forward. "I just —" She broke off. "I don't want to talk about it. It's personal. And don't you go blabbing, either."

I just — Had Tobi been about to say she just did it for the first time? With Jason? Karen studied Tobi, while Tobi studied the board.

Liz came in. She'd showered; her hair was wrapped in a towel. "Doughnut holes, anybody?" She held out a box from the bakery.

"You're going to get fat," Tobi said.

"And you're going to disappear one of these days if you don't start eating like a normal person." Liz leaned on Karen's shoulder. She smelled of shampoo and lemon skin lotion.

Karen moved her pawn, hoping it was a decent move, and ate a doughnut hole.

"Look, look what you did, Karen!" Tobi said. "That was dumb! You opened up your queen-bishop. Liz, I have to teach you to play this game. Karen is hopeless."

"Come on, Tobi, don't take it so seriously," Liz said.

"What other way is there?" Tobi bent over the board, pulling at her lip. "You missed the fireworks this morning, Liz. Mom and Dad got on me about Jason."

"Dad, too?"

"You betcha. Real united front. It's just pure prejudice, because Jason's older than me. I call that narrow-minded."

"Well, maybe they'll get used to the idea," Liz said.

Tobi made her move and Karen was in trouble. Tobi sat back. "He's not an ordinary person. He's an artist. Probably a genius. People like Mom and Dad ought to be falling down on their knees in front of somebody like Jason!"

"I don't think you'll get them to do that," Liz said. "But, Tobi, you know how you are — don't rush into anything —"

"Oh, God! I can't stand it. You sound just like the parents. I don't get you, Liz. I really don't. Why do you always play it so safe?"

Liz's freckles brightened. "You call quitting my job safe? You call writing poetry safe? I guess our ideas about safety are pretty different. I don't know where you get this idea that you're the only one who can do things, Tobi."

"Did I say that, Miz Liz?"

Karen moved a knight.

"What'd you do that for?" Tobi said. "You have to move your king. You have to think when you play this game, damn it."

"Leave her alone," Liz said.

Karen sprang up, knocking over the chessboard. "Stop your damn arguing. Just stop it!"

Ten

"Daveeey. . . ."

"Daveeeey," he mimicked.

"My sister's going to be home any moment."

"Which one?"

"Tobi."

"Invite her in." He tried on a leer.

"She says you're too young."

"Oh, just for that —" He kissed her again, a really fat kiss, big, sloppy, and wet. She knew him — he did it just to be annoying.

She wriggled free. "Davey, remember our first kiss?"

"Total novices. I remember bumping your nose and being so embarrassed."

"I guess we've learned a few things since then."

"I don't know about you, but I have."

"How do you rate yourself?"

"Off the chart."

"He said, modestly."

"Well, look, Karen, if a thing is so, it's so. We

60

could give lessons in kissing. We've had plenty of practice, since we don't hardly do nothin' else."

"You are so subtle."

"Do you have anything against sex?"

"David." She tried for a heavy dose of irony in her voice. "I have nothing against sex. I'm a card-carrying member of the majority party — I approve of it."

"So?"

"So, it still doesn't mean I want to do it — the ultimate — immediately."

"How do you know that?" he demanded. "How do you know you like steak or don't like steak if you've never eaten it? If you never had ice cream, wouldn't you be dumb to be sitting around here saying, Oh, no, I don't want to have any ice cream, that's not for me."

"I don't think we're talking about the same things," she said. She wished she got as worked up as he did. It would make life easier. She was so tired of saying no and feeling in the wrong. Right then, in the middle of his big speech about steak and ice cream, he was also shoving one hand under her sweater and fiddling with the elastic of her pants with the other hand.

"What clever hands," she said, grabbing for them. Useless to be subtle with Davey. He was slippery as an eel, had at least ten hands and twenty different approaches. She finally settled for the basic defend-yourself approach and pushed him away.

"Very nice," he said. "What am I, on your Enemy Number One list?"

"I know your hormones are churning," she said, trying to be amusing. "It's typical of teenage males."

David didn't look amused. No wonder. She didn't think it was very funny, either. "You know, Davey — David! — I want to say something. It really makes me feel punky to be always putting on the brakes."

"So give it the gas." He threw himself down on the floor.

She stepped over him. "What makes me feel punky is to always be the cop."

"So, stop," he said, staring up at her.

"You look like a dead person." She picked up a little statue Tobi had given her years ago, something she got by sending in boxtops. A little pink and green plaster shepherdess with an innocent look on her sweet, dopey little face. "I guess I'm not making myself clear," Karen said.

"You know, Karen, I want to say something to you, too." He closed his eyes, put his hands over his chest like a corpse. "Did it ever occur to you," he said in a deep voice, "that maybe you are too young for me?"

"That's very suave of you, Davey."

"Now don't get mad, I just want to talk about this."

Karen stared at the cover of a fashion magazine. Liz must have left it in her room. Who was this fabulous creature on the cover, her hair flowing out behind her, smiling at her as if to say, You see how easy it is to be a woman!

"Talk about what, Davey? We're exactly the same age; in fact, I'm a month older than you."

"I didn't mean literally, age-wise."

"Oh, God," she said, sounding like Tobi. "What are we talking about here?"

"Don't you know?"

"Would I ask if I did?"

He rolled over, kicked his feet. "Oh, well . . ." he said in a muffled voice. He sat up. "Forget I said anything."

"No, come on. If you want to talk about something, let's talk."

"Forget it, forget it, forget it," he said rapidly.

They went downstairs to the kitchen, sat down across from each other, and went to work on a carton of peach ice cream. "Did we just fight?" she said.

He shrugged. The hum of the refrigerator. The scrape of spoons in the ice-cream carton.

Finally, she said, "Do you want to come over to my grandmother's with me?"

"Why?"

"I promised I'd visit her this week, bring you along."

"How'd I get into this?"

"She wants to meet you."

"Look me over, see if I'm okay for her Karen?"

"Something like that, I guess. Come on, be a pal. My grandma's liable to send me to Siberia if I disappoint her. Or strangle Gladys Goldfish."

"I'm always your pal," he muttered. "Aren't I always a gooood boy?"

"God, Davey."

They took the bus over to her grandmother's. Karen toted Gladys in her plastic bag and David had Eggbert in a sling he'd made out of an old sock. Some people stared at them. She poked Davey and wriggled her eyebrows. He wriggled his in return, but half-heartedly.

Her grandmother lived in the Sudbury Towers,

63

a semi-fancy apartment building. They took the elevator to the fourth floor. "Creaky old thing," Davey said, and gave the wall a hard kick.

"Maybe we shouldn't go, after all," Karen said. "You really are in a foul mood."

"Uh-uh. You didn't drag me all the way over here just to call it off. We're visiting Grandma."

She rang the bell. "Karen?" her grandmother said, then opened the door. "To what do I owe this unusual pleasure?"

Kiss her cheek. Introduce Davey. Go inside.

Her grandmother's apartment was small, but elegant. Lots of shining, polished wood, brocaded chair seats, and velvet curtains. She had on a turban that matched her curtains, deep green with a sparkling jeweled pin set in the middle.

"That is a great turban," Davey said.

"Why, thank you, David." She passed him a plate of little frosted cookies. "Take plenty."

"I hope we didn't come at a bad time for you, Grandma."

"What could be a bad time for me, Karen? An old lady like me has nothing but time on her hands and nothing to fill that time."

A reminder that Karen was in general a crummy, neglectful granddaughter?

David examined a picture on the wall. "Who're these women, Mrs. Freed?" He sounded intelligent and respectful.

"Those are women I employed in my shop."

"What kind of shop was that, Mrs. Freed?" Oh, what a pussycat. "You designed your own hats? Where'd you get your ideas? Did you ever sell a hat to a famous person? Did you make men's hats,

64

too?" He sounded as if Grandma's having a hat shop was just about the most fascinating thing he'd ever come across. Before long, Davey and her grandmother were chatting away like two old best buddies.

Suddenly Karen heard her grandmother say, "Oh, no, Karen isn't very curious."

She sat there, hurt, stunned. Was it true? She thought of herself as full of questions. Big questions, important questions, the questions of her life!

"David," her grandmother said, "you have more the makings of a reporter than a biologist."

"Oh, I'll report the doings of the frogs and the mosquitoes." Her grandmother laughed as if she hadn't ever been quite so well amused.

"I'm sure I say funnier things," Karen said after they left. "And I never get her to crack a chuckle."

"The old Kursh charm."

"He said, modestly."

"Karen, when a thing is so, it's — "

"I know, I know."

"I like your grandmother. She's kind of a grand-old-lady type."

"Right." The whole afternoon depressed her. That weird fight-no-fight with Davey. Then the visit with Grandma. Pretty clear that her grandmother preferred Davey, an utter stranger, to her. That hurt. "She's awfully formal. Didn't you think so?"

They stopped on the corner near the bank to wait for the bus. "What I think is," he said, "if you don't get along with her, it's your own fault."

"Just what I need, Davey. A little honest criticism." But it hit home. She found herself explaining how her grandmother was never interested in her.

65

"She's always telling me to work hard in school. And saying how brilliant my father was. That's her whole conversation with me. She's different with Tobi and Liz. Well, everybody is fascinated by Tobi, anyway. And Grandma likes Liz because Liz is beautiful and —"

"Karen, get off it. The way you talk about your sisters — it's really sick!" He stuck his face in hers. "Sure, Liz is beautiful. She's super beautiful. And Tobi, I'll take your word she's fascinating and smart. Maybe she's a genius. So what? What does that make you? Nothing? Maybe you're just jealous of your sisters, Karen."

"Excellent! Thank you! This has been an outstandingly wonderful afternoon. You don't like anything I do, you don't like anything I say. I mean, it's just been the same thing the whole bloody afternoon."

"Hey." Davey held up his hands. "Say no more." The bus was coming, his bus, but he walked away and disappeared around the corner.

Eleven

Saturday morning, Karen threw some fruit and cookies in a bag, put her camera around her neck, and wheeled her bike out of the garage. The front tire was flat. She pumped it up and yelled good-bye again to her mother, who'd come outside to dump the garbage. Karen didn't mean to do it, but found herself on Davey's street. She bent low and pedaled fast past the little grocery store.

Going out of the city, traffic was heavy. It was a perfect spring day and the farther she got from the city, the bluer the sky. She was nearly to Paradise Lake when a red pickup truck slowed and pulled over. Scott looked out the window. "Karen!"

"Hi." She straddled her bike.

"What are you doing way out here?"

"I was going over to Paradise Lake."

He leaned on his arm. "Where the hell is that?"

She waved. "About a mile on."

"Oh, you mean Mud Pond."

"Mud Pond?"

"It's where you're going."

"No. Paradise Lake."

"Same thing," he said. "You're not swimming in this weather?"

"I just wanted someplace to go. What do you mean, Mud Pond and Paradise Lake are the same?"

"Oh, I'll tell you about it," he said. But then he didn't, just leaned on his arm, smiling and looking at her.

She put her hand up to shade her eyes from the sun. "Well. . . ." Was the conversation going to die right here? Then she thought, Ask him where he's going. "Where're you going, Scott?"

"Out to the house we're building."

"Oh, it's out this way?" Then she thought of something else to say. "The one you were showing Liz? You're going to work on it?"

He looked sheepish. "No, I was just going out to admire it a little. Want to come along with me and see it?"

"I don't know. . . ." Liar. Of course she wanted to go with him. What if he was just saying it, though, only being nice to her so he could impress Liz? *I took your kid sister out to the site, showed her around, cute kid. . . .*

"We can throw your bike in back." There was a big red tool chest in back of the pickup, some empty boxes, and scraps of wood. "Plenty of room," he said. He started to get out.

"No, I can do it."

He got out, anyway, and it ended with both of them lifting her bike into the back of the truck.

She climbed into the front seat.

"I like to show off everything I do. I'm not modest

at all." He lit a cigarette. "The house is on Robert Kelly Road, Karen." He held out the pack to her. "Do you smoke?"

"No. But I'd like to have one, anyway." She lit up, blew smoke and tipped her head.

"I'm not too good at inner solitude," Scott said. "I'm the sort of person who likes company better than being alone. How about you, Karen?"

"Yes, I'm the same." Was she? She puffed away.

"You go swimming at the lake a lot?"

"Not so much anymore. A few times every summer."

"I bet you're a good swimmer. You look like you have swimmers' shoulders. I used to swim there when I was a kid, when it was Mud Pond." He put his hand briefly on her knee. "That was before your time."

"You really called it Mud Pond?"

"Oh, sure. We'd swim from one shore to the other. It was smaller then, you could swim all the way across and feel like a big hero. Big Olympic stuff. But every time you got out of the water, you had to do a leech hunt."

"Ugggh, leeches."

"You ever pull leeches from in between your toes, Karen?"

"We used to kill them with salt."

"Try a lit cigarette."

"Uggggh. I hate them."

"Uggggh. Me, too."

He pulled out the ashtray. "Here's the ashtray, Karen."

She tapped ash, put the cigarette back between her lips.

"When Marvin Paradisio bought the pond, first thing he did, even before he bulldozed it out, was put up NO TRESPASSING signs to keep us kids off. And then he built that phony entrance with the turrets and towers."

"You don't like it?"

Maybe her distress was apparent in her voice. Scott patted her knee again. "It's kind of cute, campy, but you know I was brought up on good old plain Mud Pond." He slowed down. "There it is."

Over the years the sign had gone gray and faded.

" 'Welcome to Paradise Lake.' Some welcome," Scott said. "You have to pay to get in, don't you?"

"Not that much. It used to be just a quarter."

"And now?"

"Well . . . seventy five cents last time I was there. That was last year."

"Probably be a dollar this year." Scott laughed. "A buck to swim in Mud Pond! What a crazy world."

But it was worth it! Worth it to Karen to see the same woman, in the same little booth, who'd been there the day Liz got her license. Thin, dark-eyed, sticking her bony claw out of her cage, the woman took your money and gave you a key without a word. Always it was the same thing — the woman, then the sagging wooden decking, the bare dressing room, the showers that spritzed little streams of cold water on the damp cement floors, and hanging over everything, over the hot, dirty sand and the little lake, the spicy odor of hot dogs, like the smell of summer.

The house Scott was building was a few miles past Paradise Lake, on top of a hill. The house was framed up, the roof trusses in place. Below, the land

70

rolled away. Karen looked off at the land and the the sky, thinking that there were some things you couldn't photograph, some things you couldn't even speak about.

"Ready to see the house?" Scott had a roll of blueprints under his arm.

She followed him up a wooden ramp. Light fell into the house everywhere. "That's going to be a wall and there'll be a skylight there," Scott said, pointing. "Maybe a fireplace. This is going to be the master bedroom . . . window here, looking into the woods. . . ." They went up a ladder to look at the loft area. "Wood, plus solar heat. You know what the insulation is? R-16." He unrolled the prints, spread them out on the floor. "I love showing this place off."

"You really are more like an architect," she said.

"No, what I know I've picked up here and there. I was carpentering when I was twelve years old with my dad. You learn a lot that way."

They sat outside on the framed deck, shared Karen's fruit and cookies and a candy bar Scott fished out of his jacket. She put her camera down next to her.

"Liz says you do a lot of stuff with photography, Karen."

"I just fool around. I like it, but. . . ."

"What sort of things do you photograph?"

"I don't know. Faces. Hands. Feet."

"Feet?"

She looked at him from the corner of her eye. "I have this theory, sort of, that you can tell a person's character from their shoes."

He stuck out his feet. "Get out your crystal ball."

She aimed the camera at his feet. He was wearing muddy, stub-nosed work boots with red and white laces. "You have enthusiasm, you're hard-working, but you also have fun in life."

"Right on the mark." He hugged her, the camera between them, his face against her face. A warm, firm hug. Her voice dried up, she smelled metal, cigarettes, soap. And what if he said to her, Come on! Give me a little kiss!

They started talking again, as if it were completely ordinary that they were there together. Well, it was, wasn't it? Karen couldn't stop thinking about the hug and his skin and the smell of his skin, as if they had crept into her, were becoming part of her. "Yes, that was funny." They were talking about a movie. Apparently she sounded normal. But she couldn't stop thinking about his arm so close to her arm, his leg so close to her leg. . . .

"Are you cold, Karen?"

She must have shivered. "No. I'm fine."

He rolled up the prints and they went back to the truck. Karen got her bike. "Glad to give you a ride back into the city," he said.

"Oh, no, that's all right." They shook hands, a formal moment, as if the hug never had been. He climbed into the truck, waved, and drove off immediately. She stood there only a moment, then she left, too.

Twelve

Karen tied a red and blue scarf around her neck and fastened three silver ear clips on her left ear. Some other touch was still needed. Yesterday in school, Davey had been very stagey about not noticing her. From which she concluded that they were still fighting. *She* wasn't mad anymore. In fact, she was in a wonderful mood, had been ever since Saturday and Scott. She put on a hat, a fedora that had been her grandmother's, tipped it over her eyes and picked up Gertrude.

In the kitchen she took a banana and sat down across from Tobi. "Hel-lo!"

Tobi raised her hair off her face, grunted, and let the hair drop again. Tobi was always only half human in the morning until she ate something. Then Karen remembered last night. Jason had driven Tobi home from school — or somewhere. As her mother had said, confronting Tobi in the hall, "Surely school doesn't let out at ten to eleven."

"Very fine sarcasm, Mom." Tobi had walked into

the living room, where Karen was eating grapes and watching tv.

Her mother followed her. "Where were you?"

Tobi popped a grape into her mouth. "With Jason."

"Yes, I heard that much. Someplace where there was no phone?"

"As a matter of fact, you're right. No phone."

"Ahh. And where is this primitive place?"

Tobi chewed the grape and breathed hard. "Jason's studio," she said finally. "He can't have a phone ringing when he's working."

"Jason's studio. Is that where he lives, too?"

"As a matter of fact, yes. We ate supper there."

Her mother studied Tobi, seemed about to say something, then walked out. But a moment later she was back. "There must have been a phone somewhere!"

"I'm sorry I didn't call. Next time I will call you. All right? Can we end the inquisition?"

"No. One more question. Why did he drop you and run?"

"He didn't drop me and run! He knows he's not welcome here."

"Where did he get that idea? Did I ever say that? Did your father?"

"Mom. Everything does not have to be said in order to be understood."

Through all that, Karen hadn't said a word, although she felt she ought to show her loyalty to Tobi in some way. Now, in the breakfast nook, in a voice loud enough to reach her parents in the dining room, she said, "I'd like to see some of Jason's sculpture, Tobi."

Tobi, grateful creature that she was, only grunted. So much for gestures of solidarity.

Karen's father gave her a lift to school. Last year he'd bought himself an English car, a white Rover with low-slung red seats. "Maybe I'd learn to drive faster if I practiced on your car, Dad."

He downshifted tenderly at a corner. "No, darling."

"Mom's car is so clunky."

"There's only one key to this car and —"

"— it's in my pocket," Karen finished with him. He dropped her at the corner near the school. She gave him a kiss in payment for the ride, although she hadn't liked kissing him for about a year now.

In school she saw Marisa and ran to catch up with her. "Hi, Marisa, I'm in a fabulous mood."

"You look it! I like your hat."

"The last time I wore it, Mr. Radosh had a fit. He wanted to take it away from me. I just said, No, no, no, no, no way, dear Mr. R. I must have been in a fabulous mood that day, too."

"There's your friend," Marisa said, as Davey walked by with a group of boys. He glanced at Karen and then pointedly away.

"What was that about?" Marisa asked.

"The big D and I had a fight the other day."

"Oh, it can't be serious?"

"I don't think so. We'll make it up."

She was jaunty all day. She and David finally came face-to-face in Mrs. Pritchard's science class. Talking to Tommy Taylor, he stood with his arms folded across his chest, hair falling in his face.

"Hiii," Karen said.

"Hi, Karen," Tommy said. Nothing from Davey.

She sat down at her desk with Gladys. Behind her, someone yawned like a sea lion. Chester Mills slumped at his seat, his long face down on his arms. She started planning a series of photos. High school. But it wouldn't be happy, happy yearbook stuff, it would be gritty, real . . . dirty pipes in the basement . . . water on the bathroom floor . . . tired teacher faces . . . sullen student faces. . . .

"Hi, there." She stuck her foot across the aisle toward Davey.

"Mmm." Davey glowered. Roar. Roar. The lion in his den.

"How's Eggbert doing?"

"Mmm."

She tipped her hat down over her eyes. "Mmm, mmm," she mimicked. Oh, well, now that she'd started, she wasn't about to give up. "Say, Davey, your kid looks a bit grubby. He could use a bath."

"He's a slob."

A real sentence. "Sorry for you, Dad. My kid, now, she's a four-star bather."

"Good old Gladys."

"Well, today's the day we can turn our kids out of house and home if we want to."

"About time, too. Little Eggy is getting the boot right into the garbage."

"You're not going to miss the child?"

"If you want to know the truth, he's starting to stink."

"I guess I'll keep Gladys for a while." She tapped Davey's foot. "So, are we friends again, or what?"

"Why not?" he said.

His lack of enthusiasm hurt. Maybe that was the

point — he was still mad. She leaned her head on her hand, thought again about trying to get across to Davey how she felt. Put it in simple words. I like you. I like you a lot. More than any other boy I know. I like kissing you. That's great. I mean it. The rest of it — can't we just wait?

They met after school with some other kids to play touch football. She left her hat under a tree and borrowed a sweat shirt from Tommy Taylor. The grass was soggy; they ran, passed the ball, slid, and slipped. "Get him, Karen," Tommy yelled, "get Davidface." She tackled him, the ball popped out of his hands, Margie Lewis grabbed it, and Karen and Davey fell to the ground together. "Hi, friend," she said to his muddy face.

He gave her a hand up, pursed his lips, and said fast, "Karen, I've been thinking. We should stop going together."

"What?" she said, although she'd heard him perfectly.

"Stop going together," he repeated softly. "Okay?" he said. "Okay?"

Billy Parker yelled, "Hey, hey, hey. Heads up, guys." David held out his hands for the ball, it sailed past him and then everyone was running, screaming, and Karen heard herself say, "Okay. Okay, if that's what you want, Davey," and she turned into the pack of kids, running with them.

Thirteen

I n the little bathroom off the kitchen, Karen washed the mud off her face. Her eyes kept leaking tears. The knees of her jeans were stiff with mud. She stuffed them in the hamper and went into the kitchen. She was incredibly hungry. She slurped down a dish of slimy tapioca, ate the rest of the stale butter cookies, and peeled a banana.

The mail was on the counter. Bills, catalogues, magazines, and a single letter, an oversize sky-blue envelope addressed to Tobi. On the back flap, the return signature: Jason Wade Wilson. Then Tobi's name scrawled across the face of the envelope in green ink, looped and full of flourishes, as festive as a bunch of green balloons sailing into a blue sky. Karen thought, If Davey wrote me a letter, it would have a black border and disappearing ink.

She threw the banana peel into the sink. It was full of dishes; the morning pots were still on the stove. She stared at the mess. Her mother would come home and say, "Why didn't you wash the dishes? Scrub potatoes for tonight? Set the table, at least! Doesn't anybody do anything in this house but me?" Karen stuck her fingers into the jam jar, licked them. How come Liz hadn't cleaned up? Or Tobi? Both so dopey in love they didn't even see what was under their noses?

She picked up the letter, traced her fingers across Tobi's name. A love letter. You could tell just from the way Jason had sent Tobi's name flying across the envelope. That, in itself, was a love message. She thought with a kind of awful despair of how much Jason must love Tobi.

Karen had never had a love letter from anybody. Certainly not from Davey. Now and then a note passed in school, a few words scribbled on a torn piece of paper, none of them memorable. "Can U meet me at trophy case? . . . Dr. B. gave me 1 hr detention. . . . I need 2$, pay you back Fri." A man of few words. With a few words, he'd broken them apart as easily as snapping a stick in half. And she, the original cooperative kid, had meekly and sweetly agreed. Okay, Davey, if that's what you want. Her little voice. Her reasonable voice. Why hadn't she screamed in his face? You traitor! No, it's not all right, turkey dip! It's all wrong! We're friends! Friends don't act this way!

What if he was already regretting it? What if he was home right now writing her? His first real letter to her, the most important letter of his life.

Dear Karen, Is it too late? Are you still speaking to me, or have I ruined everything? I don't know why I said what I did. Of course, I don't want to break up with you! I think you're fantastic. You're the best friend I ever had. So whatever I said today, just forget it. Love, D. P.S. You can call me Davey from now on, if you want to.

Dear David, I just this minute got your letter. Thank goodness! I was horribly hurt, David. I cried when I got home. I know we have our differences, but I always thought we would go on being friends, no matter what. So, no, it isn't too late. It's never too late for friends like us. Love, Karen.

She was still ferociously hungry. She looked in the refrigerator, rummaged in the cupboards. Fudge — that was what she wanted. She melted butter, dumped cups of sugar and cocoa into a pot, stirred and tasted. Only fudge so chewy and sweet it would make her teeth ache and her father howl could satisfy that gnawing in her stomach. She poured the dark liquid mixture into a pan to cool and sat down with the pot scrapings.

Davey was a fool for fudge. Maybe she should call him up and invite him over for a fudge party. She reached out for the phone, dialed his number, then hung up in horror. What was she doing! Where was her pride? Her backbone? Where was all that anger? Was this the way she told him off?

Tobi came in, her face red and sweaty. She drank a glass of cold water, then took a tiny fleck of fudge from the pot. "Better destroy the evidence before Dad gets home."

"You got a letter, Tobi. On the cupboard."

Tobi tore open the envelope.

"Why did Jason write you? Doesn't he see you at school?"

"Every day." She allowed herself a smile, then went to work on a sandwich. A light coating of mustard on a slice of bread, a paper-thin slice of cheese, then enough lettuce to feed a hutch of rabbits.

"Aren't you going to read Jason's letter?"

"Not here. No offense meant."

"Tobi — do you really love him?"

"You're not going to start on me, are you?"

"I wouldn't!" Karen felt hurt. Tobi knew she was loyal.

Tobi sat down at the table and picked up the newspaper. "What's Brenda Starr up to today? Oh, poor Basil, he's got himself into trouble with his sister, Anise."

Basil! Brenda Starr! Anise! Karen was ready to scream. She told herself, Don't say anything about Davey. Tobi doesn't confide in you, why blab to her? And the next minute, she said it. "Davey and I broke up today."

"Ohhh." Tobi squeezed her arm. For a moment tears came to Karen's eyes at Tobi's sympathy. "Look at her face," Tobi said. "Look at that face." Then she had to ruin it. "Karen, he gave you the heave-ho?"

She pulled away. "Tobi! What a rotten way to put it, like I'm some kind of old garbage."

"No, I didn't mean that. Don't be —"

— so sensitive, Karen finished, scraping back her chair so she wouldn't have to hear the words. She shoved a chunk of fudge into her mouth, tasted the melting sweetness going down her throat. This was terrible. She felt so sorry for herself! She scored the fudge in the pan with a sharp knife, down and

81

across, like a chess board. Or Davey's heart.

After Tobi went upstairs, Karen kept eyeing the phone. Would it be so terrible to call him? What was the big deal about pride, anyway? Saving face? Wasn't that half the trouble with the world? If more people could just say, "Hey! What are we fighting about, anyway?" wouldn't the world be a much better place to live in? Suppose the Soviet Union and the United States could get together like that? *White House to Kremlin. Just made a pan of terrific fudge. Come on over and share.* The Premier and the President scraping the pan out together. But how was that supposed to happen if people like her and Davey couldn't even make up their troubles?

Suppose she called, said hello? Kept it cool and friendly. Just checked out the situation. She reached for the phone again. "Karen, what you are doing is okay," she reassured herself, listening to the phone ring in Davey's house. He wasn't home yet. Or . . . he was in the bathroom, washing off the mud. Or he was with another girl. Oh, the rat! One more ring and that was it. He'd just have to miss out on the fudge.

"Hello?"

"Oh! . . . Hello Davey."

"Karen?"

"Did you just get home?"

"Yeah. You?"

"A while ago. . . . I just made fudge."

"Yeah?"

"It's cooling now."

"How'd it come out?"

"Good."

With that, the conversation died. They both

82

breathed for a few moments. Not that different from fifty other conversations of theirs. Ordinary and nice. Had she imagined everything? The touch football game and the mud . . . Davey's voice. . . .

"Davey? Why did you say that?"

"What?"

"You know —"

"Karen, you said okay. You agreed."

"I didn't have much choice. . . . Don't panic, I'm just asking you why."

"Well, you know, don't you?"

"I'm asking, Davey. If I knew, I wouldn't ask."

"I want out, Karen."

"I figured that part out, Davey!"

"Listen, Karen, you're making me say it —"

"Say it. Say it. I don't give a damn!"

"We don't see eye-to-eye on certain things."

"Things? What things? Eye-to-eye? What does that mean? Could you please explain yourself?"

"Karen, do you have to talk like a machine gun?"

"Thanks, Davey, I'll always treasure the memory of your tender words."

"Don't be so sarcastic, Karen."

"Sarcastic! I'm not sarcastic. I'm just pretty *upset*. You gave me quite a surprise today. An actual Sunday punch! Somebody I've known and been close to for two years pops up in the middle of a game with a little message for me. By the way, Karen, we're not friends anymore. . . . That kind of stuff can be confusing, Davey. So, now I'm just trying to find out why. I wouldn't have called you otherwise. Believe me, I wouldn't have bothered you, Davey. Not for the world!"

"Look, Karen, the best way I can tell you is that

we've hung out together too long. Nothing was happening. The same old stuff all the time. Even the same old arguments. It was getting boring! BORING."

"Oh," she said.

"You made me say it."

"That's okay, Davey. You're right. I made you say it." She hung up.

In the middle of the night, Karen bolted up in bed, seeing Davey's smile when he gave her the kiss off, the old heave-ho. Seeing that toothy white smile, ashamed and gloating, as clearly as if it were floating over her head.

It was no use trying to go back to sleep. She got out of bed and went downstairs. There was a light under her mother's study door. She rapped. "Mom?"

Her mother was at her desk, writing on a yellow pad. A cigarette burned in the ashtray. "What are you doing up, sweetie?"

"I couldn't sleep. Maybe I'll make cocoa."

"I couldn't sleep, either. It must be the full moon or something." She patted her lap for Karen to sit down. "Want to talk?"

"I don't know." Karen sat in her mother's lap. "Davey and I broke up." Her voice wobbled. She hadn't meant to say anything.

Her mother didn't seem surprised. "You feel really bad about it?"

Karen shrugged and moved uncomfortably. She was so huge to be sitting on her mother's lap!

"Maybe it was time for it to happen," her mother suggested. She stroked Karen's hair. "You know, just because Davey initiated the break-up —" But how did she know that, Karen thought, unless Tobi had told her? "It's not always good to be so exclusive, Karen; you cut yourself off from a lot of interesting people —"

She went on in this vein, but Karen only half listened. What right did Tobi have to talk behind her back? *Mom, guess what, old Davey gave our little monkey the heave-ho.*

She picked up the yellow pad her mother had been writing on. "Marjorie Quaker's new book, *The Stars,* is a comprehensive survey of —"

"Karen, put that down, please."

She went on reading the review. "Very well written, Mom. But a little obscure right in the middle." She was giving her mother her honest opinion, no bland pats on the back, nothing *boring,* an honest, insightful comment.

Her mother reached for the pad. "Karen, you know what my rule is on reading things before they're pub —"

She jumped off her mother's lap, holding the pad out of reach.

"Please give that to me," her mother said.

Karen continued to hold up the pad, away from her mother. A peculiar, pleasing warmth filled her stomach, as if she'd just eaten a bowl of hot oatmeal: the spreading, satisfying warmth of being a bully, the one who shoves other people around. For once, the kiss-off-er, the rude heave-ho-er, not the pathetic heave-ho-ee. "Why do you have that rule?"

"I don't happen to be very secure about what I write."

"Why? Why is that? Why?"

Her mother's face flushed. "Give that to me! Just

because you don't feel good, Karen, is no excuse for taking it out on other people."

"I don't know what you mean. I just wanted to read your stupid, boring little review!"

Her mother took off her glasses and looked at her without speaking, a look like Tobi's, a cold, ferocious look that could kill.

Say something, Karen told herself. *I didn't mean it, Mom. Your reviews aren't stupid. They're not boring. It's me, Mom.* She dropped the pad on the desk, pulled the cord on her bathrobe tighter, like pulling a cord around her neck. In the face of that look, she couldn't speak, couldn't apologize, couldn't take back the words.

Fourteen

Karen lay on her belly under the mulberry tree, listening to the rise and fall of Liz's and her mother's voices. They were strolling through the yard with their arms around each other, their voices twining together like the buzzing of flies. Karen liked lying there listening to them. She and her mother had sulked at each other for a day or two, then made up their quarrel. First her mother had smiled ruefully at her. "Are we going to talk?" Then they hugged and Karen said, "I'm sorry," at the same moment her mother said, "We were both tired."

Now her mother and Liz were talking about having a vegetable garden this summer. "There's nothing like getting your hands in the soil," her mother said. "In my next incarnation, I'll be a gardener."

"But who's going to do the work? Scott says —"

Karen rolled over. *Scott. . . .*

"— he'd have a garden, but —"

. . . sitting next to him in the truck . . . looking at the blueprints. . . .

"— he did enough weeding when he was a kid."
. . . *then the hug.* . . .

She looked up at the sky through the branches of the tree. Blue, blue sky. . . . *blue skies smi-iii-iling at meee.* . . . How could she feel so bad about Davey still and yet go on thinking nonstop about Scott?

It had been such a weird week. Seeing Davey every day and not exchanging a word, a glance, not so much as a sneer. It was as shocking as opening a favorite book, a story you knew by heart, to find nothing there but empty pages.

Her mother called over, "Karen'll do our weeding, won't you?"

She leaned up on her elbow. "I won't have time to weed. I'll be working."

"Working." They both looked at her. "This is the first I've heard of that," her mother said.

Surprise. It was the first Karen had heard of it, too. "Yes. In a diner, maybe . . . or maybe a store in the mall." She was improvising. She had no idea, hadn't done anything about finding work. She didn't even know she was thinking about it until she said it. Maybe Scott would hire her. Qualifications? I took shop. I can hammer nails, use a band saw. I'm strong and willing to work. I'll learn anything you want to teach me.

On tv, she'd seen a woman construction worker. The woman's boss had said, "She's a good worker and we all like her." At night the construction worker took off her hard hat and became a photographer's model: lacy dresses, long eyelashes, posing with her hair blowing in the wind.

At lunch, Scott and Karen would sit on the deck

sharing their sandwiches. At night she would take off her hard hat and they'd go some place for a cool drink. They'd sit next to each other on stools at a counter, their legs touching, and talk over the absurd and serious things that had happened on the job that day. Every once in a while she'd remember Davey and laugh lightly. A light laugh of amusement. . . . Maybe she'd mention him to Scott. Lightly. Ironically. Oh, yes, she'd say, my adolescent love life. . . .

Monday, on the way out of school, Marisa and she ran into Davey. "Hello, Karen."

So, they were speaking again — by Davey decree. "Hello, Davey." She meant to be cool and didn't succeed. "You know Marisa —"

"Hi, there," he said to her, holding the door open.

"Ever the little gentleman," Karen muttered.

"That's me." He was wearing faded jeans, a green scarf around his forehead, a baggy blue sweat shirt, probably to hide the role of fat around his middle. What a mean thought. If she paid attention she'd probably find out she had mean thoughts every hour on the hour. At least.

Marisa flashed him a smile. "David Kursh, aren't you in my chem class?"

"No, you're in my chem class."

"Well, I've heard many things about you."

He laughed uneasily. "What have you been saying about me, Karen?"

"I never bad-mouthed you, Davey." But she didn't mind that he was sweating a little.

He walked down the steps with them, maneuvering to get between Karen and Marisa. "I've been meaning to ask you, Karen. I don't suppose you still want to go to the Army Ants concert next Saturday?"

"Davey, I don't suppose you want to go with me. Somehow, someway, I picked up that idea."

His ears flushed gently. "Well, I have the tickets. Besides, I asked you to go — I don't break my word —"

"Their lead singer is intense," Marisa said.

"Totally," Davey agreed. "Did I tell you I've been doing some stuff for your grandmother, Karen?" Talking to her, but looking at Marisa. "Washing windows, running errands. . . ."

"The strangest thing," Marisa said suddenly. "You remind me so much of someone, David. A boy I knew when I lived in Paris. Tony."

"Tony? Doesn't sound very French to me."

"Oh, no, there are French Tonys. But you're right, he wasn't. My Tony was English."

"Your Tony — so I remind you of him?"

"Yes. Something about you — maybe your voice."

"Good-looking chap?"

"Very."

"And how'd you meet this fine-looking English lad?"

"He came to Paris to visit a friend of a friend."

"And —"

"Oh, she was busy, so I was assigned to show Tony all around Paris."

"I'm jealous."

Karen looked from one to the other. What was she doing here? Spectator? Referee? Dating service? Fifth wheel, that was it. The two of them began talking about Carrington, the chem teacher. "I like it best when she stands up on the desk to get our attention," Marisa said. "American schools and American teachers are so funny. You would never find anything like that in France."

From Miss Carrington and France, they went on to discuss the Big Topics. Life. Plans. The Future. When Davey heard that Marisa wanted to go to med school, he got so excited he stepped on Karen's feet. "Marisa, this is really something!"

"Off my feet, fat man," Karen said.

Davey sidestepped. "I'm interested in biology, Marisa." He was off and away on his favorite topic — the schools he might go to, possibilities in the field, his hope of working in a lab over the summer.

"And so on and so on," Karen said. Then to Marisa, "Actually, this is Davey's second favorite topic."

"What's his first?"

"Three lettters. One guess."

"Freed, what's your problem?" Davey said.

"Davey, this is BORING, I've heard it all before."

"Freed, why don't you leave?"

"Kursh, why don't you give Marisa a chance to say something? Marisa, I'll just go on ahead —"

"No, no, Karen, I'm coming." Marisa linked arms with her. "Ciao, David."

The next day, Davey, who for the last week couldn't have found Karen in a crowd of one, spotted her instantly in the bedlam that was first lunch in the cafeteria. "Where's your friend?" He put his tray down.

"She has second lunch."

"You know what would be great? What if I could shuffle up another ticket to the Army Ants concert? Then we could all go together."

"Davey, I've been thinking about it. Marisa can have my ticket."

"Oh, no, Karen."

"Why not, Davey?"

"Karen —" Sincere, concerned frown. "I don't want you to miss the concert."

"It's okay."

"No, no." Firm, hearty, masculine tones. "I can't let you do that."

"You can let me do it, Davey."

"Karen? Honest?"

"Honest."

"Well . . . if you're sure. . . ."

"I'm sure, Davey," she said. "I'm sure."

Fifteen

Marisa and Davey went to the Army Ants concert on Saturday night, then for a walk Sunday morning and to an afternoon movie, something called *The Gods Must Be Crazy*. Marisa reported all this to Karen, Sunday night, over the phone. "Davey wanted to see this movie. It was wonderful. Very funny. And the concert, I'm sorry you missed it, Karen."

"Big social life," Karen said, and thought of Marisa and Davey side by side in the dark theater, Davey's laugh rolling out. He had a laugh that was a laugh in itself. Har-har-har, like a friendly dog barking. She imagined Marisa's head on his shoulder.

"Karen? I like you both so much, I don't want to get between you."

Karen lay on the floor in the upstairs hall. "Don't worry, please, there's so much space between Davey and me, the whole U.S. Marine Corps could get in there and you'd never notice."

"Well, if you're sure —"

93

"I'm about ready to hang out my shingle, Marisa. Karen Freed, Matchmaker."

Monday in school she saw them together near the trophy case on the first floor, the same place she and Davey used to meet. There they were, her ex-boyfriend and her best girl friend, bumping into each other, their heads close, and there she was, walking on by alone. As the song said, All by her lonesome.

Since she couldn't have a social life and she couldn't have a boyfriend, she decided she'd have a job. Forget love. Concentrate on money. She assumed she would land a job right away, the way she landed a fish the first time her father ever took her fishing. She'd been seven, never so much as held a pole in her hand, threw in the line and was hit immediately. Instantly! A two-pound big-mouth bass. Her father was ecstatic. She couldn't understand why he was so excited, until it never happened to her again.

That beginner's luck must have imprinted her. She thought all she had to do was stroll into a store or two, announce her intention to work (throwing out the line) and flip flop, the big fish would land in her boat. Well, not quite. Every place she went, they already had their summer help ("But leave your application, if you want to; it can't hurt"), or they had no plans to hire anybody ("But fill out an application; things might pick up"), or they wanted someone older. Or someone more experienced. Or someone who could work night hours.

The closest she came was in a doughnut shop, a tiny place, barely big enough for the counter and the tall, skinny boy behind it. A neat row of pimples was tattooed across his forehead. He wore whites and a name pin. KEVIN MASON. "Help you?" he said, doughnut tongs at the ready.

"I'd like to speak to the manager, please."

"You got him." Kevin pointed to himself.

"Oh. I'm looking for summer work."

He leaned on the counter. "I bet you think it would be fun working here surrounded by doughnuts? Let me tell you, after a couple of days you'd be happy never to look another doughnut in the eye." He waved at the heaps of doughnuts in the bins behind him. "I loved those things before I came to work here. Especially chocolate doughnuts. I could eat two or three chocolate doughnuts a day. Just give me a chance and I'd do it. I'd eat a chocolate doughnut first thing in the morning, I'd eat one before I went to bed, and then I'd get up in the middle of the night and eat another one. You know what I mean?"

"You were a chocolate doughnut freak."

"Exactly right. I came to work here and was I happy to get this job! One, I needed the money; two, I could eat all the chocolate doughnuts I wanted every day. You want the truth? I'll give you a statistic. I've worked here a year. In the last ten months, I haven't eaten a single chocolate doughnut."

The door opened and three men came in and sat down at the counter. Kevin Mason glanced over at them. "Be right with you, gentlemen." After he served them, he came back to Karen. He leaned toward her confidentially. "Did you see that? They all ordered chocolate doughnuts. I'll tell you the truth. I don't even like to look at the little suckers anymore. So what's your name?"

"Karen Freed."

"Okay." He scribbled it on a piece of paper.

"Don't you want me to fill out an application?"

He shrugged. "I've got your name. Here, put down your phone number." He pushed the paper toward her. "We'll call you if we get an opening."

"Should I check back?"

He smiled; his pimples brightened like a row of neon lights. "You want the truth? I wouldn't mind. But we don't need anybody. Not unless I drop dead or something."

By Friday, she couldn't stand the thought of making the rounds of yet another mall. She played soccer after school, kicking the ball as if it were Davey's head. "Way to go, Karen!" her teammates yelled.

On the way home, she stopped in at a sporting goods store in the mall to do some shopping for Tobi who, being Tobi, wasn't content to say, "Buy me three pairs of white socks." No, Tobi's white socks had to have a yellow stripe, be ankle-length, and at least eighty-percent cotton.

It took Karen about fifteen minutes to pick out Tobi's socks and another five to find a pair of shorts for herself. She got in line with her packages and there, two people to the front of her, was Scott. He was wearing a blue shirt with the sleeves rolled up. She reached around, touched his shoulder. "Scott?"

"Hey, Karen! What are you doing here?"

She held up her packages. "Cotton socks. What about you?"

He held up a single leather glove. "Racquetball."

"You're wearing a tie today."

He looked down as if surprised. "Yeah, I am."

The people between them looked back and forth as if they were at a tennis match. Scott left his place in line, came back to stand with her. She hopped from one foot to the other, cracked her knuckles loudly, and rubbed her nose, which had begun itching furiously. "Good grief," she whispered under her breath.

She began talking too fast, machine-gun style. "Buying anything for Tobi is big business. Tobi — you do something for her and she makes you feel she's doing you a favor. The same talent as my grandmother. Know what I mean? The two of them — they're such characters. . . ."

"Yeah." He smiled, his hands in the pockets of his cords.

Yeah? What did that mean? She stared at him suspiciously, felt disloyal to her sister and her grandmother. It was his turn at the register, then hers. She paid and was humbly astonished that he was waiting for her.

They left the mall together and gradually she calmed down. "You're not working out at the house site today?" she asked. A normal question! Dull but normal.

"One day a week I work in the office, try to catch up with things."

"Oh. The tie! What sort of things?"

"You don't really want to hear."

"No, I do, I'm interested."

"Well, the nasty part of 'things' is calling people who are trying to stiff us on their bills and talking tough. I try my best to sound like a dues-paying member of the Mafia. Pay up or else —"

"— kneecap job."

He laughed. "The nice part of 'things' is getting down to some of the design work."

She thought about asking him for a job. "I've been looking for work." Maybe he'd think of it himself.

"Any luck?"

"Lots of it. All bad. It's sort of discouraging."

They stood by his truck. "I could drive you around to a few places before I go back to the office."

"Really? You'd do that?"

He shrugged. "Why not?" He looked at his watch. "I don't have to be back right away."

She got into the truck. He lit a cigarette. "Can I have one?" He passed her his and lit another. Filthy taste. She didn't know how people got the habit. She loved tapping the ash, though, and then holding the cigarette to her lips. "I heard a woman talking on public radio about the art of cigarette smoking," she said.

"People have funny ideas. You shouldn't get the habit, Karen. In fact, I feel guilty about letting you do this." He reached out, took the cigarette from her, and mashed it on the floor.

"Well, hell," she said, but her heart wasn't in it. Could we do that again? You light up. I ask for a cigarette. You take it from your lips and give it to me. Then you take it away. After that, you light another cigarette. I ask for a puff. You take it from your lips. . . .

He pulled into the parking lot of a restaurant. "Try this place, Karen. I heard Grimaldi's was one of the best restaurants in town to work in."

She went in. It was the usual routine. "I'm here to apply for a job."

"Nothing now." The manager was tall and fat. "Leave an application."

She turned thumbs down as she got back in the truck. "Bummer," Scott said. The next place was the same thing. And the next. And the one after.

"We should count up the ways people say no, Karen."

"Sorry," she said promptly. "Nothing now. Come back in a month."

"Don't bother coming back at all."

"Leave an application. Don't leave an application. We're not hiring inexperienced help. We only want people with experience. You're too young. I thought you were older."

"Maybe you'll get into the *Guinness Book of Records*, Karen."

"Karen Freed, turned down seven hundred and fifty-nine times for jobs in the space of one hour, and no two turndowns exactly alike."

"It sounds like a winner."

They stopped to have doughnuts and coffee. Sitting at the counter, Scott said something about Jason's "problem."

"You mean his ego?" Karen said.

"That, too. But I was thinking of the drinking."

"What drinking?"

"Don't you know? Am I talking out of line? Liz said something about it, so I thought you all knew."

It was stupid of her, but the first thing Karen thought was not how bad for Tobi to be mixed up with a drinker, but that her sisters had their little secrets from her. Again. Or was it always? The two of them, the older two, whispering together. Of course she was too young to know something so terrible! Couldn't possibly handle it. Might go into shock.

Scott dunked his doughnut. "From what Liz said, it's a letting-down thing, a weekend thing. I knew a guy like that in college. Straight arrow all week, then kaflooey, totally blitzed every weekend."

In the truck again, he said, "One more place, then I really have to get back." He pulled up in front of a little store. "You want to try this place?"

She leaned forward to look at the lettering on the window. HAMMAR AND SAWYER CONSTRUCTION CO. "Your office! You need someone?" she blurted.

"What? Oh! I'm sorry, Karen, I didn't mean — it was just a joke."

"No, that's okay." She was embarrassed, talked fast. "Can I see it? The office? I really want to see your office."

"Hey, it's nothing special."

The room was cluttered — two desks, a drawing board, a huge metal filing cabinet, a scattering of chairs. Scott showed her some plans he was working on. "It could be a big job if the client likes what I come up with. . . . Is this boring for you?"

"No, I'm not bored, no, not at all."

"You won't hurt my feelings."

"Never with you," she blurted. Good grief, good grief. . . .

"Sweet." He kissed her on the cheek.

At home, she didn't say anything about meeting Scott. *Oh, by the way, Liz, I was buying socks for Tobi and guess who I met? . . . Yes . . . and then he drove me around to look for work. And we stopped in his office.* What was so hard about saying that? Why didn't she say it? *He showed me plans for a house he's going to build. I'm sure you've seen them. . . .*

Did he kiss you?
Only on the cheek, Liz! Just a quick little kiss.
Sort of a peck. Really. Like an uncle or a
brother. . . .
Maybe not tell Liz at all. Try it out on Tobi first.
Who would roll her eyes. *He kissed you on the*
cheek? Oh, biiiiig deal! Or would she? Tobi knew
what it meant to want something — someone — no
one else wanted you to have. She was still seeing
Jason, probably more than ever, but she couldn't
even bring up his name without starting a ruckus
in the family. For a while it had been mostly their
mother, but even her father had gotten on her case
now.

"Tobi, darling. . . ." The other day, going past
Tobi's bedrooom, Karen had heard him talking in
that slightly spaced out, patient way of his. Telling
Tobi what she already knew. That Jason was older,
more experienced, had been married. "Your relationship is not appropriate." To everything, Tobi
had barely replied. "I know. . . . That's right. . . .
Uh-huh." At the time, Karen had felt a little sorry
for her father because he was so sincere about wanting to straighten out Tobi, but now she didn't blame
Tobi one bit for stonewalling. Appropriate? Tobi
was in love.

And Karen? She wasn't ready to go that far yet.
But, still, was it that much different with her and
Scott? The family would laugh if they knew he'd
kissed her. They wouldn't take it seriously, not one
of them, not even Tobi. Laugh, she thought. Go
ahead, all of you. But I'm not laughing. A brotherly
kiss? For him, maybe. But me, I wish he'd kissed
me on the lips, that's what I really wish.

Sixteen

Saturday, Karen was in the cellar loading the washing machine when Liz called her to the phone. "Hello?"

"Karen, this is Patty of Patty's Pretties on Jordan Avenue. You put in an application for work. Can you come down for an interview today? Say, in about an hour?"

"All right." She hung up and panicked. Jordan Avenue was all the way across town. And Patty's Pretties? She hardly remembered it. Maybe one of the places Scott had taken her. "Liz! Will you drive me somewhere?" How lucky Liz wasn't working today! She ran up to her room, pulled on a skirt, pinned up her hair to look older, then earrings, lip gloss, a touch of blush.

"What kind of a place is it?" Liz said, in the car.

Karen craned her neck to inspect herself in the mirror. "I don't know. It might be a little jewelry place."

"Jordan Ave. is over near where Scott lives."

"Mmmm." *She and Scott are celebrating her new job, sitting across from each other in a booth, their feet touching under the table. He leans toward her, touches her hand. I can't talk to anybody else the way I talk to you, Karen. . . .*

You can tell me anything, Scott. . . .

I know. Karen, darling. Neither one of us wants to hurt Liz, but what can we do? . . .

"Drive a little faster, Liz."

"You don't have to be there at an exact moment, Karen."

"My first real job offer, I don't want to flub it."

"Try to be calm. Breathe deep, that helps."

"Do I look all right?"

"You look fine. Relax."

The warm weather had everyone out in the streets. Packs of dogs roamed around, kids were playing softball. A couple of boys were laid out like fish fillets on top of a car, reflectors held to their faces.

Liz pulled up in front of the store. "Well, good luck."

It wasn't a jewelry store, after all, although it had some jewelry. It was more of a variety store, selling scarves, greeting cards, all sorts of little knickknacks and gifts. She walked through a cloud of hanging chimes to where a woman in a long white dress was dusting the glass counters.

Karen smiled nervously. "I'm Karen Freed. You asked me to come down to see about the job?"

"Right, Karen. I'm Monica, but when I'm here,

you call me Patty." She looked Karen over. "Can you go to work immediately, Karen? I need someone to start Monday."

"Monday? Well . . . no. I'm in school."

"I thought — how old are you, Karen?"

She cleared her throat. "I'll be sixteen on my next birthday, Moni — Patty. . . ."

Patty or Monica flicked the dustcloth over a display of glass animals. "You're big, that makes you look older. So — you're still in school."

"Yes, I'm looking for a summer job. Do you need someone for the summer?"

"I'm sorry, I really want someone full-time."

In the car, Liz patted her knee. "It took me ages to find my first job, too." She turned a corner. "There's Scott's street, let's go see if he's home."

"Hawthorne?" Karen said, sitting up.

"The next one over, Oak. You've been over to his place with me."

"No." Karen looked out the window.

Oak Street was mostly two-family houses with porches up and down. Scott was out on the street washing the pickup truck, bare-chested, wearing faded gray shorts, a pair of rubber clogs.

They got out of the car and crossed the street. Liz tiptoed up behind Scott and grabbed him around the waist. "Ooof!" He turned around. "Well, both of you are here — great. Look at you, Karen. All dressed up."

"Doesn't she look nice?" Liz said.

They went up to his apartment. He lived on the second floor. The stairs were narrow and Karen walked behind him and Liz. They walked into the living room. A big room. A long, green couch, a stereo on the floor, a couple of easy chairs. In the kitchen Scott brought out beer and soda. Liz seemed familiar with everything, went into the little pantry off the kitchen for crackers, put cheese on a plate, took out knives from a drawer.

Scott took a long swallow of the beer. He'd put on a shirt. "I thought you were poeming all day today," he said to Liz.

"That was the plan but — you know . . . and Karen needed a ride. . . ."

"No flow, huh?"

"Oh, it was okay for about half an hour. Then I got stuck on a word, one single stinky little word. A skunk of a word."

Scott smiled at Karen. "Ordinary people like us don't have those kinds of problems. So you got called for a job, Karen?"

"Yes, but it was a mistake —"

"I ought to write a poem about skunky words," Liz said.

"— she thought I wanted full-time work," Karen finished.

"A-ha, we add that one to our list," Scott said.

"What list?" Liz looked from Karen to Scott. "What's so funny?"

"Karen and I are putting together a new list for *The Guinness Book.*" Scott told Liz about driving Karen around to look for work.

Liz tapped her mouth. "I didn't hear about that."

"No. I forgot to tell you." Karen picked up the soda, finished it in one gulp.

"You know what I was thinking, Liz?" Scott

draped his arm over Liz's chair. "I'd really like to get a dog."

Liz was still watching Karen, still tapping her lip. Was she thinking about her poem? A poem about skunks and words? Or a poem about skunks and sisters?

Seventeen

Liz's freckled fingers tapped the wheel in a little dance. "Do you think we've waited long enough?" Her hair was loose; she was wearing a pale green dress. She looked like a sea goddess, all green and gold and dappled.

Karen cast a sidelong glance at Liz. She hadn't forgotten that sister-skunk look Liz had shot at her last week. As soon as Tobi showed up, Karen decided, she'd give up the front seat. For once she wouldn't mind sitting in back and letting Liz and Tobi have each other all to themselves.

"Let's wait five more minutes," she said, craning her neck out the car window. Had Tobi forgotten that they were all supposed to meet their parents at the New India Restaurant for dinner? A double celebration: Karen's father's birthday and her parents' anniversary.

"I say, let's go," Liz said. She hated being late for anything. She backed out of the driveway.

Since that afternoon last week in Scott's apart-

107

ment, she and Liz had not been alone together. And now here they were, in about as cramped quarters as you could get, stuck together in Liz's little VW bug. Karen wriggled uncomfortably in the seat. One way or another, she realized, she had managed to avoid close contact with her sister for days. That was odd! She'd been acting guilty. But of what? And why? She hadn't done anything — as long as you didn't count thoughts.

They drove in silence. The restaurant was north of the city, all the way out on Route 11. "What a funny place for a restaurant," Karen said finally. "Far far out in the boo-boo-booonies."

Liz smiled faintly. Karen smoothed her skirt, checked her fingernails. Her hair was up again. Twisting the clip through it, she remembered Scott's saying, You're all dressed up! He was coming to dinner, too. *Don't think about him.* An impossible command.

"It's a new restaurant," Liz said. "Somebody, one of Scott's customers, mentioned it to him."

Why had Liz said *Scott* in that odd tone of voice? Or had she sounded perfectly normal? Put those questions in the paranoia question box.

Sometimes Karen couldn't tell what Liz was thinking. Correction. Most times. Liz was beautiful like cool dappled water and that was what you saw, not the bottom, not the sandy, gritty, stony, rough stuff. Which was probably why that sister-skunk look on her face had impressed itself so on Karen. Now Tobi — she showed everything on her face. You always knew if she was mad, sad, glad, whatever.

As for her, Karen, what was it Marisa had said

to her once? "Karen, give yourself a rest. You think too much about every little thing. With you, everything is chewed up."

"Like dog biscuit," she'd agreed.

Why couldn't she accept things? Let them happen, let them be whatever they were going to be. What was it that old Beatles song Tobi liked so much said? *Let it be, let it be.* For instance, in a little while she'd see Scott. That was nice. No reason to fall apart. She could handle it. A smile. A few words. Hello, Scott. Nice to see you. Six easy words. After that, relax, lean back, don't say anything. Silence was admirable. Scott would notice how quiet and thoughtful she was, he'd look at her, that quiet, sympathetic look as if the two of them were completely in accord. . . .

She jerked upright. She was doing it again . . . fading out, falling into a satisfying fantasy about Scott, and with Liz right next to her. Had Liz just said something? She glanced at her sister. Some people were supposed to be super sensitive to thoughts. They could tune in. What if Liz were one of those? What if she was tuned in to everything Karen thought? Or, more to the point, tuned in to everything Karen thought about Scott?

What she had to do, Karen told herself, was concentrate on something else, put Scott right out of her mind. Watch the white line in the road. Notice the color of those reddish bushes in the ditch. How about that faded sign they'd just passed in front of a farmhouse? PIK UR OWN STRAWBERIES. In April? Those people would never win a spelling contest, either. See how easy it was. For at least five minutes she hadn't given Scott one stray thought.

"Oh, good, here it is," Liz said.

The New India Restaurant was a plain white building, set in the middle of a field like a barn. Beyond it, a line of yellow willow trees. A cow bellowed. Another car turned into the lot behind them. "There's Mom."

"I knew she'd be on time." Liz locked the car. "Scott should show up any moment."

"What about Jason? Is he coming?"

"I don't think Mom invited him."

"Oh! Tobi's not going to like that."

Their mother came up, combing her hair. Her blouse had pulled out of her skirt. "Hi! Am I late?"

"You can't be late, you're the guest of honor." Liz tucked her blouse for her.

"Where's Tobi?" Their mother peered into the VW. "She didn't come with you? She didn't come home from school?"

"Mom, let's go in," Liz said. "Maybe she's here already."

She wasn't. The restaurant was cool, dim, and nearly empty. Pink tablecloths, the gleam of silver, bud vases, each one with a single pink carnation. A man with dark, smooth black hair bowed. "Follow me, please." Refined English accent. They sat down and another man poured water.

"We'll have a bottle of the house white wine," her mother said. She glanced at her watch. "Grandma's coming with Daddy. He could have picked Tobi up, too. What is she up to? In some ways, she's so scatterbrained —"

"Tobi?" Karen said. "Mom, she's not —"

"Well, not scatterbrained, but you know what I

110

mean," she said, turning up her hands in appeal to Liz. "Just sort of — hectic?"

Liz laughed. "Yeah, Tobi's hectic, all right."

Karen drew patterns in the tablecloth with a fork. Maybe Tobi was with Jason. In his studio? She imagined it big and bare, white walls and lots of windows on the north side. Artists liked northern light. She'd always wondered why. There'd be a skylight, too, and a bed right under it so he could look up at night and see the stars. Besides the bed, maybe just a few chairs. And his easel, of course. No, not an easel; he wasn't a painter. What did sculptors work with? Clay? Patting little balls of clay the way they used to when they were kids? Karen had never been any good at that; the only thing she could make were snakes. Maybe he was working in marble. She could imagine him in his jeans and desert boots climbing up the side of a hunk of marble, chipping away at it with a hammer. And Tobi? Where was she in this picture? Sitting on a chair, gazing up at Jason admiringly? Uh-uh! That wasn't Tobi's style. Washing his dirty dishes at the sink? Scratch that one, too. Try again. This time, the picture that popped into Karen's head was of Tobi and Jason together on the bed beneath the skylight.

"Hello," her mother said. "You found it all right."

Karen looked up. There was Scott, his hand on Liz's shoulder, smiling around, at her mother, at her. She hadn't even seen him approach. He wore a light blue shirt, blue and gray striped tie. Karen stared at him, stunned, half of her still in that big white loft with the skylight.

111

"Hello, Mrs. Freed. Happy anniversary," Scott said. He sat down next to Liz.

A few minutes later her father and grandmother showed up. Her father a little rumpled, his shirt creased, his tie loosened, but her grandmother, as usual, elegant in a soft brimmed hat, a velvet dress with a jeweled flower spray brooch at her neck.

"Grandma, you look beautiful. You could be a model," Liz said.

"Thank you, sweetheart."

"You all look beautiful," her father said.

"Daddy, how courtly."

Her father looked around the table, humming and polishing the top of his head, that little bald patch — no wonder it was so shiny. "So we're gathered here to celebrate our anniversary. Imagine that. Twenty-three years."

"And your birthday, Arnold," Grandma said. "A little late, I might add." His birthday had passed the week before.

"Twenty-three years, that's really something," Scott said. "That's really special." Liz and he were holding hands.

"Well, if you two make it official, a real engagement, you could have a shot at something just as good. Not that I'm saying it's easy to make a good marriage and keep it going."

"Hear, hear," her mother murmured.

"You need patience and you have to know how to compromise. Anything good isn't come by easily," he ended. A long speech for her father.

The talk went here and there, what her mother called chitchat. Karen was thinking her own thoughts, or maybe not thinking at all, just feeling things. She and Scott happened to be sitting directly across from each other. She only had to stretch her leg to touch his foot with hers. In a movie she'd seen, a man and a woman who were each married to someone else had carried on practically an entire love affair beneath a dinner table, and with a dozen other people present. They'd touched each other, given each other little nudges and pats; their hands had talked a special sign language. And all the time, above the table, they carried on normally, talking and laughing with the other people.

Suddenly Liz said, "Karen? Your face is all red." Boom! It was as if a piece of the ceiling had dropped into the middle of the table. All talk stopped. Five pairs of eyes turned on her. Karen's face is red! What can be the matter! "Maybe you're getting sick?" Liz said, and she reached across the table to touch Karen's forehead.

"Don't!" Karen jerked away. She was horrified. Liz was treating her like a five-year-old. She pushed away from the table.

"Karen?" her mother said after her. "Are you all right?"

Yes! No! Leave me alone! In her haste, she bumped into a table. Were they all still watching? In the women's room she locked the door, shoved her wrists under the cold water, splashed her cheeks and her lips. *What's the matter, Karen? Your face is all red.* Tears of rage gathered behind her eyes. She slapped her hands against the side of the basin, slapped them again and again, stinging them, bruising them.

When she came back, the waiter was at the table with the bottle of wine wrapped in a napkin. Her mother glanced at her, but to her relief no one said

113

anything. The waiter poured wine into a glass and handed it to her father. He raised his eyebrows at her mother and said, "You want to do it, Syl?" Karen's mother laughed; she sipped the wine and nodded. "Very nice." The waiter, smiling, filled the rest of the glasses.

"Here's to twenty-three more years," her father said, holding up his glass.

"No, Arnie, let's not toast until everyone's here. Tobi —"

"We'll make more and better toasts when Tobi comes. Right now I'm toasting us. Twenty-three terrific years."

"They haven't been bad," her mother said.

"That's the best you can do?"

"They've been pretty good." She kissed him.

Eighteen

When Tobi finally showed up, she was in jeans and running sneakers, a scarf tied around her forehead. Not dressed for a party at all. "We waited for you —" Karen began, and her mother pushed out a chair, but Tobi held up her hand.

"I'm not staying. I just came to say, Mom and Dad, congratulations on your anniversary, but if you can't invite Jason, who is my friend, to this party, then I don't want to be part of it, either."

Karen's face flushed as if *she'd* said those words, as if she were the one so upset and upsetting everyone else. Tobi was brave. Wonderful!

"Tobi —" Her mother half rose. "Please, we're all here. We want you with us."

"No!"

"Tobi, sit down," her grandmother said, puffing up like a rooster. "What is this nonsense?"

"Mother," her father said, "this is between —"

"At least Grandma's not a hypocrite," Tobi cut in. "You guys don't even try to know Jason. You're just prejudiced against him because of his age. That is so narrow-minded."

Karen glanced at Scott. He had moved his chair slightly back, slightly away, as if to say, Don't mind me, I know I'm not part of this.

"Jason is outside now?" her father said. "He's here?"

"Yes. He drove me. I wasn't even going to show up! But he said I shouldn't do that to you. That's the kind of man he is. He wasn't invited, but he's not small-minded."

There was a short silence. "Well . . . since he is here," her mother said, "why don't we ask him to join us?"

Tobi quivered like a wound-up spring. "Oh, no! Oh, no! Last minute invitation? I'm not doing that to Jason." Her eyes filled. "Oh, damn —" And she was gone.

Karen went after her, running between the tables and catching up to Tobi in the entrance. She was on her way out. "Tobi!"

She paused, half in, half out. "What do you want, Karen? Did they send you after me?"

"No, Tobi! Don't you think I can make up my own mind? I think you're right, Jason should have been invited."

Tobi's eyes were bright with tears. "Thanks, Karen, at least somebody in this family —"

"Tobes— "

Tobi waited.

"I just —" She shook her head. "I mean, I —" She knew what she wanted to say. *I admire you, I think it's wonderful the way you do things. You make up your mind what's right and stick to it. But*

116

it was easier to think than say. And just then, anyway, Liz came rushing up.

"Tobi." She put her arm around her sister, closed the door, took over the situation. "Come on, kiddo, get Jason and come back to the table. Do you want me to get Jason? Listen — it's their anniversary."

"Liz, no."

"Mom's really upset, Tobi, she feels terrible about this whole thing."

Tobi grimaced. "You always take Mom's part."

"Come on," Liz coaxed, "don't be stiff-necked. What's it going to get you?"

"She's not stiff-necked," Karen broke in. "Tobi's got principles."

Tobi opened the big wooden door. The air smelled faintly of spices. The three of them stood together in the doorway. "No, it would be so insulting to ask Jason now."

"She's not coming back?" Karen's mother said when she and Liz returned to the table. Karen thought she looked ready to cry.

"You spoil your girls," Grandma said. "I told you that a long time ago, Sylvia."

"Why don't we order?" Liz opened the oversized red menu. "Who knows Indian food? Mom, you're the resource person here, what are chapatties? They sound like cowboy boots."

"It's a kind of Indian bread," Karen's father said. They buzzed back and forth about what to order. Her father began a story about one of his patients whose fillings were receiving UFO reports. Her mother laughed, but still looked downhearted.

Karen's shoes were pinching her and she slipped them off. Why did they have to pretend? What was so great about carrying on as if nothing were wrong? Something was wrong! This was a family gathering and Tobi wasn't with them. Karen looked at Scott. He wasn't taken in by all the false jolliness! He sat there soberly, studying the menu, quiet, not saying anything.

The dinner seemed to go on interminably. Tobi was right about one thing — Grandma was no hypocrite. She had two more remarks to deliver herself of, and she did. "Everything is too spicy," she announced in the middle of everyone else's praising the delicious food. "I've eaten in Indian restaurants far superior to this one." And after that, "I still don't understand Tobi's disgraceful performance."

Her father drove her grandmother home; Karen went with her mother. She got in the car, buckled her seat belt. Scott and Liz were standing by the VW, their hands on each other's shoulders. Karen closed her eyes. The whole evening had been awful, her family was awful, she hated them all, she didn't leave out a one of them. Liz's reaching across the table to touch her forehead . . . Grandma's brusque pronouncements . . . the mess with Tobi. Awful. Awful. Her mother started the car; it jerked forward. As they turned out of the parking lot, Karen looked back. What had she expected to see? Scott walking away from Liz? Liz yelling at Scott? Something unreal like that. What she saw was Scott and Liz kissing, their arms around each other so tightly they looked like one person.

Nineteen

Two things happened right after that, just days later. They didn't have anything to do with each other, except that they happened on the same day. They were both sort of shameful and awful, only the first thing was worse for Karen and the second for Tobi.

Tuesday morning Karen was rummaging in Liz's bureau for a pair of underpants. She'd waited for Liz to go into the shower. She might be wary of being around Liz, but she still liked wearing her underpants, which were a small miracle, always looking good, silky sweet colors of pink and soft green, no rips, no mends, no tears. Whereas, by some evil chance, Karen's underpants seemed to metamorphose into a totally ratty state only days after she brought them home from the store.

She took a pair of green underpants. Then she noticed a T-shirt folded in the corner. Why did she pick it up? Why that one? Why not another one? Did she know what she'd see? She shook it out. Blue, with the Hammar and Sawyer logo printed across the front. She couldn't remember ever seeing it before.

She took it. She took the T-shirt. She walked out of the room with it tucked under her arm. She went down the hall, past the bathroom, the sound of the shower, past her parents' room, into her room and closed the door. She sniffed the T-shirt like a cat. Had Scott worn it, then given it to Liz? It smelled only of fresh laundering, soapy and that warm smell of the dryer. She crumpled the T-shirt into the back of her closet, her heart beating like a thief's. She was a thief. She had stolen Liz's T-shirt. Or had she borrowed it, like the underpants? No, she had stolen it.

Later, when she and Tobi left the house, Tobi asked Karen if she wanted to come to a showing of Jason's sculptures at the college after school today. "It's an opening, a big event. Are you interested?"

"Is Liz coming?" Her voice was too bright, false, a thief's voice.

"No, she's working. And I'm not asking Mom, you can count on that."

They stood at the bus stop together. "Yes, I'd like to."

"Good." Tobi squeezed her arm.

Karen met her sister at the college library and they walked over to the Emma Farrington Gallery together. Today it was given over to Jason's sculptures in metal, wood, plastic, and even paper. A small crowd of people moved through the gallery. There was a table with a punch bowl, plates of cookies.

"Jase is somewhere around here," Tobi said.

"I never saw so many beards in one room," Karen said.

"Faculty."

The gallery had half walls dividing it into several smaller rooms. Tobi went off to look for Jason, and Karen walked around, pausing in front of each sculpture and reading the little printed white cards. "Gayle, 1984." That in front of a small, contorted piece of wood. "Mysteries." Three brass plates strung one above the other on a copper pipe. People passed in front of the pieces, whispering respectfully, cupping their hands in their chins, nodding, murmuring.

A man behind her said, "Buy him now," and a woman answered, "I give him five years and then the cover of *Time*."

Karen's ears pricked up. So they thought Jason was going to be famous, too. She kept trying to eavesdrop, to pick up a clue that would tell her what she was supposed to feel about Jason's sculptures. Mostly she felt bewildered and bored. Then she turned a corner and received a shock. An enormous piece of rough hewn stone thrust itself toward the ceiling. Not the marble she had imagined Jason rappeling up, but some kind of granite, gray with red and blue threads. It was both noisy and quiet. It was rough, crude, and yet made everything else in the gallery laughable — the plates of cookies, the whispering people, Jason's other works. It was as if a piece of a mountain had burst through the window, demanding to be noticed and yet left alone. She walked around it happily. The card on the base read, "Voices From The Other World," and reading it, Karen experienced another little burst of pleasure centered right in her belly, as if she'd known that was what it was called. It couldn't be called anything else.

Tobi came back. Karen grabbed her arm. "Look at this! Look at this!"

"I know." Tobi caressed the granite. "Now do you understand?"

They went into an adjoining room. Jason was there, looming over a little cluster of women. "You need someone to take the daily burdens off your shoulders," a woman in a lavender jump suit was saying. She smiled modestly, as if she were ready instantly to offer herself in the role of burden-taker.

"Jason." Tobi raised her hand. Jason looked up; his glance slid from Tobi to Karen, then away. "Well, I'm thirsty," he said to Lavender Jump Suit. "I'm heading for the refreshments. Anybody got anything to spike them with?" The women, like bodyguards or maybe a harem, closed around him as he walked out of the room, his desert boots clanking over the tile floor.

Tobi stood there for a moment, pale as paper. Karen moved close to her. "Tobi —"

"Don't say anything."

On the bus home, Tobi sat by the window, staring out. "He could have said hello," she said at one point. "At least hello."

Karen wanted to touch Tobi, but the angle of her shoulders was sharp and forbidding. And she couldn't think of anything comforting to say. Jason was a rat. That was what she wanted to tell Tobi. He's a rat, a dirty rat! She didn't understand how someone who was an artist, maybe even a genius, someone who could do things with a piece of stone that made you want to cry and laugh with happiness — she didn't understand how such a person could also be your basic crud.

That night she took Scott's T-shirt out of the closet, laid it across her pillow and slept on it. In the morning she put it back in the closet. She didn't know why she'd done it, why she'd done any of it — taken the T-shirt, kept it, slept on it. She brushed her hair, heard Tobi clumping down the hall. Her hand froze in midair. Poor Tobi! Then she thought there was one thing she did know. As far as men went, Liz was a thousand times luckier than Tobi.

A few afternoons later, Karen was home alone when the doorbell rang. It was Jason. "Tobi's not here," she said, standing in the doorway, remembering the gallery, not liking him, not liking him one bit.

His eyes in that browned, leathery face looked red and smaller than she remembered. He leaned against the door frame. "So you're —" He snapped his fingers. "Ah — the kid sister."

"Karen," she said shortly, and repeated, "Tobi's out right now."

"Well, I'll just wait for her." And without Karen's knowing how it happened, he was past her and inside, in the hall and ambling toward the kitchen. "Where's the rest of the gang? You home all alone?"

She didn't like that question. "They'll be home any minute. Look, I don't think my mother would like you to —"

"Relax, kid sister, I'm not going to throw you down on the floor and ravish you. Get me a beer, will you?" But in the kitchen the awful man opened the refrigerator himself. "What the hell kind of a house is this," he said amiably. "Only two bottles of beer. A house without a goodly supply of beer, kid sister, is a house without character, is a house without imagination, is a house without hospitality."

He took the beer into the hall and sat down on the floor — no, really, what he did was a kind of enormously graceful, deliberate slide down the wall to the floor where he hunkered, tipping the beer to his mouth.

And what was she supposed to do — leave him there for whoever came home to stumble over? Carry on a polite conversation? Go about her business? She stood indecisively, leaning against the little triangular phone table. He had left her speechless, outraged and, to be truthful, both fascinated and frightened. Those last two in about equal parts. He was so large and so unpredictable. He didn't act like ordinary people. She eyed the phone. In an emergency, call your operator. Operator! Operator! There's a beer-drinking bear loose in my house.

It was her house. Her hall. Her terrain! How had he managed to make it seem that she was the intruder and he the laird of the castle, relaxing in his own way. He set the bottle down and hummed, low, deep in his throat, his eyes unfocused, staring off as if he were an aborigine sitting in front of a campfire, humming and mulling over the day's business.

Karen's scalp prickled. The man was strange. She had the sensation of something unseen, indefinable but real, of an aura surrounding him and reaching out to touch her, to touch everything in its path. An energy that was strong, powerful, radiant, arrogant.

After a while she went upstairs. Tiresome standing over him like a prison guard — not that he seemed bothered. He didn't pay any attention to her. The laird ignoring the boorish peasant. She sat down at the top of the stairs with her books. From there she could watch him. He was still hunkered down in the same place when Tobi came in.

"Hello, bird," he said.

"What are you doing here?"

"I came to see you." He put his hand up to her.

"Most people call before they come to a person's house."

"Since when am I most people?"

"You know since when." Tobi was pale, taut. She stood straight, her hands at her sides.

Sitting on the steps, Karen felt as if she were an audience of one at a play. But this was her sister, her sister who would eat her alive if she caught her eavesdropping. Karen coughed. "Tobi —"

Tobi looked up. "What?"

"I'm sorry, Tobi, he just came in."

"Tobi, Tobifer," he said. "Let's go out. We have to talk. We have a lot to talk about."

"We have nothing to talk about. Say anything you want right here. Then you can leave."

"So hard on me," he said. "Why do you care about those women? They're intellectual groupies." He laughed. "Didn't I tell you that?"

"I don't care about them. It's not that!"

"Oh, now." He sounded weary for a moment.

125

"Because I didn't say hello. But you know why, I warned you about all that, I told you about that foolishness."

"What foolishness? You have words for everything. You do what you want and then you —"

"No," he said, "you're a student. I'm a teacher, or so they say. That's why they pay me. Student. Teacher. You and me, we're a no-no-no-no-no." He stood up, almost slid up the wall as he'd slid down it. Maybe a bear, but a dancing bear. "I miss you," he said. "I've been missing you a whole lot."

"No," Tobi said.

"Yes. Yes, Tobi."

"I don't like it!" she cried. "I won't have that!"

"Tobi — it won't always be like this."

"I don't like it!" she said again.

"All right," he said quietly. "All right."

And at that moment, something changed. Karen, sitting on the stairs, wondered what she had missed. She had been waiting for Tobi to make him leave. Instead, Tobi left with him.

She hadn't come back by supper time and Liz was out, too, with Scott, so it was only Karen and her parents at the table. Heavy weather. This gave her parents a chance to concentrate on her, to ask her about school and job-hunting. They meant well, but it was all kind of depressing. Her father said he knew without a doubt — shades of her grandmother — that with a little extra effort Karen could do much better in school.

And her mother, also seeking to be positive, told her that she was sure to find a job if she kept at it. "It may be a cliché, but it's true. If at first, you don't succeed —"

"Okay, Mom," Karen said hastily. "Fine. I got it." It was true that she had slacked off in her job search.

"Where'd you say Tobi was?" her father asked.

"She went out with Jason."

He tipped back in his chair. "Ah, yes. You said so. So. She's still seeing him?"

"You knew that, Arnie," her mother said.

"I suppose I did. . . . Why did the girls have to go out on the same night? Couldn't they at least take turns? This isn't my idea of a family meal."

"Arnie," her mother said, "it just happened. They didn't plan it this way to make you unhappy. Anyway, we're lucky we still have all three of them living home. A lot of girls Liz's age, and Tobi's, too, would be gone by now."

"That's right, you guys," Karen said, "then you'd be stuck with me." But what she thought was that she'd be stuck with them. She couldn't imagine life in the house without Liz and Tobi. Yet, it was true what her mother said. One of these days, Liz would leave — to marry Scott? — and then it would be Tobi's turn to leave, and after that, hers. But if life without Tobi and Liz was unimaginable, her own life in the future was even more unimaginable.

Halfway through the meal, the phone rang. Her mother got right up. "That must be Tobi," she said expectantly, but it was an emergency call for Karen's father. He left his meal and went out. He'd only been gone five minutes when the phone rang again. "Tobi," her mother said again. But it was someone asking for a contribution to a fund to save the blue whales. "You said yes, didn't you?" Karen asked.

Her mother sighed and dug into the fruit salad. "I don't know how to say no to that stuff."

When the phone rang a third time, her mother started to get up, then sat down. "You get it, Karen." This time it was Tobi. "Karen? Tell Mom I won't be home until later."

"Mom," Karen called into the dining room. "Tobi'll be home later."

"What time?" her mother called.

"Mom wants to know what time."

"God! How do I know? Later, later."

"Mom, she doesn't know exactly when."

"Ask her where she is, Karen."

"Tobes? Where are you?"

"In a telephone booth, reporting in as requested and promised."

"Mom. She's calling from a telephone booth."

"What telephone booth?"

"Tobi? Ahhh, where is this telephone booth?"

"Tell our mother it is located next to the women's room in the back of an Italian restaurant which, itself, is located on Michigan Street next to a fairly sleazo ginmill."

"She's in an Italian restaurant on Michigan Street, Mom."

Her mother came into the kitchen, still holding her napkin. "Ask her if she has money with her, Karen."

"Do you have money, Tobi?"

"God. Does she want to know what I'm eating, Karen? An antipasto. Jason gets all the ham, but I refuse to share the olives. Is Mom right there, Karen? Why are you two playing ventriloquist?"

Karen looked at the phone, then held it out to

her mother. "Mom. Do you want to talk to Tobi?"

Her mother took the phone. "Tobes? Sweetie — you could have come home for supper. . . . No! No, I mean both of you. . . . What? . . . I mean it, Tobi. Okay, listen, we'll talk about it."

Later that night Karen woke up from a dream. In the dream she'd been in the country. She passed farms and little houses and trailers. She saw everything with great clarity. On top of a hill of ice was the house Scott was building. It had dozens of rooms. And she thought, Oh, good, right here is where I'm going. A man was hammering shingles on the roof. "I can do that," Karen called up to the man. "I'm not afraid of heights."

And at once she was on the roof next to him, kneeling down. "Here," he said, "show me." He handed her a hammer. She saw that it was Scott, after all.

That was when she woke up. And only a moment later she heard Tobi's steps passing down the hall, heard her parents' door open, heard her mother say, "Tobi?" Then Karen fell asleep again.

Twenty

Through Liz, Scott passed on to Karen a tip for a possible job. A man he had done some work for had a fruit and vegetable market, The Green Market, and might need summer help. "Scott says Derek always seems to have kids working in his market." Was that what Scott had said? Kids? Or were those Liz's words?

"It's not far from where I work," Liz said. "If you get the job, we can go to work together. Ask for Mr. Anderson."

It was a half day in school, teachers conference. Marisa and Karen met in the hall near the chem lab. "Doing anything after school?" Karen asked. "I have this job interview." Well. That sounded impressive.

"I was just going to ask you if you wanted to go shopping with me. I need a bathing suit."

"Not seeing Davey?" Karen said his name deliberately. Testing, one two three.

130

"Maybe later, if he doesn't have to work."

"He has a job?"

Marisa linked arms with Karen as they went down the stairs. "At the Veterans' Hospital, where his father is. Part time in the lab, washing bottles. Not exactly what he had in mind, but David says you have to begin somewhere."

"He has a job," Karen repeated. How irritating! And how odd to hear Marisa talking so familiarly about Davey. Odd, too, that Marisa knew more about Davey, now, than Karen did. Odder, still, that hearing his name, seeing him in school, seeing the two of them together, Karen still felt some kind of weird pang, a mixture of jealousy, anger, loss. How long was that going to go on?

The Green Market was in a renovated church, a big old white clapboard building on a narrow side street. A high-ceilinged room, long oval windows, dark wooden floors. Karen asked the woman at the counter for Mr. Anderson. A black man wearing a vee-necked sweater and cords came out of a little office. "Anderson. What can I do for you?"

She was a little taken aback by his crispness, stammered for a moment, then pulled herself together and got out that she knew Scott. "He said you might need somebody?"

"Oh, yes, I met your sister. What kind of job are you looking for, Karen? Have any experience? Cash register? Clerk?"

She looked around at the bins of fruits, a shelf with bread and thick bars of Swiss chocolate. "I'd really like to work here."

"Anybody who enjoys eating usually does."

That made her feel like a fool. A fat fool. A fat, greedy fool. And, of course, it was — Don't call us, we'll call you.

"That was quick," Marisa said, when she came out.

"It doesn't take long to say no."

Marisa pressed her arm. "You'll get a job, don't look so worried."

It was unbearable how everyone said the same inane, reassuring things. *You'll get a job. Something'll turn up. If at first you don't succeed.* . . .

"Marisa, you don't know anything about work," Karen exclaimed. Oh, that was mean! Marisa blinked, looking hurt. Karen flung her arm across Marisa's shoulders. "Don't mind me! Come on, let's stop in and see Liz, buy some jelly rolls."

Liz was waiting on a customer. Standing behind the counter, wearing a white headscarf and a white apron, she looked like a baker, herself, but the baking, the real work of The Bread Box, went on in back, out of sight. You could smell it, though, even before you opened the door to the store.

"This place smells heavenly," Marisa said when the customer left. "There aren't that many real bakeries in America. In France, they're everywhere."

"Do they really wrap the bread in newspaper?" Liz asked.

"Sometimes. And people just take it, too, without any wrapping and carry it in their string bags. Liz, do you know how to bake bread?"

"I wish I did." Liz nodded over her shoulder. "Lori, my boss, said she might teach me. . . . Any luck, Karen?"

"The usual. I left an application."

132

"Well, can I sell you ladies something? Bread? Rolls? Cake? A T-shirt?"

Karen turned away and stood in front of the tray of jelly rolls. They looked exactly the way her stomach felt, soft and squishy. Was she going to get this way every time someone said *T-shirt*? Karen still had Liz's T-shirt. If it had been only Liz's, she would have returned it by now. But it had been Scott's first. It had been touched by his hands.

"We're selling T-shirts," Liz said. "Something new. Look up there, Marisa. Karen, look, isn't that cute?" A bright yellow T-shirt with THE BREAD BOX printed across it was pinned up on the wall.

"I'll buy one," Marisa said, taking out money. Then they bought jelly rolls and a couple of oversized chocolate chip cookies, and hung around talking to Liz until another customer came in. "I really like your sister," Marisa said when they left. "She's beautiful, isn't she?"

"Yes. Everyone thinks so."

In the mall, they tried on bathing suits. Karen had decided to buy a suit, also, but she couldn't find anything to satisfy herself. The whole day had been like that. Nothing exactly wrong, nothing quite right.

She pulled up the straps of the red and blue striped Speedo she'd picked out. Marisa was trying on a sleek, dark green suit with one shoulder bare. She was a wood nymph, a forest sprite. Looking at herself in the mirror next to Marisa, Karen felt tears coming. What was the matter with her? Was she going to cry over a bathing suit? A T-shirt? A boyfriend who'd been trying to break up with her for weeks before he'd found the nerve to do it?

"Tell me, Karen," Marisa said, "should I buy it? Yes or no?"

"Yes."

"Do you think so? How do I really look?"

"Buy it." Did Marisa need Karen to tell her she was gorgeous? She had Karen's old boyfriend. What more did she want? Why be so greedy? Did Karen have to throw in compliments, too?

"I don't look too skinny in it?" Marisa held out her arms. "Chicken bones."

"Stop." Karen peeled off the Speedo.

"I wish I had arms like yours."

"STOP!" She didn't want to hear any more.

Marisa bought the wood-nymph suit. They were hungry again and went into a sandwich shop. "I left an application here," Karen said gloomily as they sat down in a booth. "I've left applications everywhere."

They had finished eating and were just about to leave when Davey showed up. "So I found you," he said, sitting down next to Marisa. "I looked all over the place. Hi, Karen."

"Hello, Davey."

"You didn't have to go to work?" Marisa said to him.

"No. Any luck shopping?"

"Ta ta!" Marisa pulled out her suit. It looked miniscule; had Karen not seen Marisa in it, she would hardly have believed it would cover her.

"Very nice." Davey touched the fabric. He and Marisa looked at each other, their faces gleaming.

When they left the mall, they split up. Marisa and Davey were going downtown, in hopes of making the science fair at the War Memorial before it closed for the day. "Come with us, Karen," Marisa said.

"No, thanks, I have other things to do." Then as she watched them walk away, she was suddenly enraged. "Marisa!" They didn't hear her. Too absorbed in each other. They kept walking. And just as well — she didn't want to go with them. But where did she want to go? What did she want to do? Who did she want to see? She didn't know until she saw the Five East bus grinding to a stop at the corner. Not her bus. The bus that went across town and all the way down Oak Street, where Scott lived.

Twenty-one

Of course Scott wasn't home. Why would he be? Karen stood on the porch, wondering, What now? Wait for him to come home? Go away and come back? Go home herself? Why had she even come here? To tell him about The Green Market. To tell him what? There was nothing to tell, and if there was, Liz could do it. An annoying thought! Slipping her knapsack off her shoulder, she tore a piece of paper out of a notebook and sat down on the top step.

"Dear Scott, I went to The Green Market today and saw Mr. Anderson. He was very nice. I left an application — this one must be 1,001! Anyway, thanks a lot for the tip. Karen."

She looked it over, not satisfied. Naturally. Nothing satisfied her today. Did she have to write him a whole letter in order to tell him one small thing? She took another sheet of paper and scribbled rapidly. "Scott. Went to Grn Mkt. Left app., no job now, maybe later. Thanx. Karen." Short, not sweet, but to the point.

She dropped it in his mailbox, then walked away, thinking about Scott taking his mail out of the box, finding her note, unfolding it, reading it. What exactly had she written? She'd abbreviated everything. Did it make sense? How had she signed it? Karen? Or, Love, Karen?

She stopped on the corner. What if Scott were there right now, reading the note and laughing, because it was stupid and absurd. The kind of note a kid would write. Kid. Wasn't that the word Liz had used?

She ran back, retrieved the note. It read as if it had been spit out by a computer. Wrong. All wrong. Why write him at all? She'd call him. But then she thought of his hands touching the paper that had been in her hands and she sat down on the steps again. "Dear Scott, Stopped by to tell you I went to The Green Market today. Mr. Anderson not too encouraging. I left an application. Thanks for the tip. Karen." She read it over anxiously. It seemed all right. Maybe she should write Love, Karen? No. It was true, but that was exactly why she couldn't write it.

She folded it carefully. Okay, this was it. A good note, she reassured herself. She was just leaving when Scott arrived in the pickup truck. She stopped, watching him park. He didn't see her until he got out of the truck. "Is that Karen?"

"Hi. I just left you a note."

He locked the truck and lifted his tool chest from the back. "A note? How come?"

"I went to The Green Market and —"

"Oh, you did. Good. What happened?" He took his mail out of the box. Her note was right on top. He read it. "So that was it?"

"That was it." She took a breath. "You wouldn't — do you need anybody to work for you?"

"Me? You mean the company?"

She nodded rapidly. "I'm not afraid of heights," she said, just the way she had in the dream. "I mean, I could do roof work, whatever —"

"I wish we were taking on apprentices," he said, "but it's not in the cards right now."

"Oh. Well, it was just an idea." She was embarrassed that she had asked. Her shoulders began to itch furiously under the straps of her knapsack.

He unlocked the door. "You want to see something? A surprise. Actually two surprises."

She followed him up the stairs to the little landing. There was a scuffling noise behind the door to his apartment, then a high whine. "Okay, boys, I'm coming." Scott opened the door and two brown and gold puppies with tremendous feet jumped all over him. "Boys, meet Karen. Karen, this is Alfred and that is Harold."

"Alfred and Harold?"

"Anglo-Saxon kings. Or do you prefer Fido and Spot?"

She bent over, put out her hand for them to sniff. You like us? You like us? Harold and Alfred cried in their big, young dog voices.

"I love you already." She got down on the floor with them. They lapped their large rough tongues all over her face and arms. "Oh, you guys, you slobs. . . ."

Scott squatted down next to her, and the dogs

frolicked around them, panting and grinning, huffing in their faces. Scott grabbed Harold, the bigger one, and rubbed his ears, then rolled on the floor with him. "Oh, he's killing me. Help. Karen, help, this monster is killing me."

He sat up and, bending toward her, he whispered, "Liz doesn't know yet that I have these guys."

"I won't tell her," she whispered back, and they both laughed.

Twenty-two

Room service," Karen said, setting the tray down on the table next to Tobi's bed. A pot of tea, orange slices, a soft-boiled egg in the baby cup.

"Oh, the baby cup," Tobi said, smiling wanly.

The baby cup was actually a small bowl with a picture on the bottom of two little girls in old-fashioned dresses. Each in her turn, Liz, Tobi, and Karen had been fed from the baby cup. Now they only used it when one of them was sick.

Karen pushed a pillow up behind Tobi's head. "Are you hungry?"

Tobi shook her head and messed the spoon around in the egg. Her face was flushed, her hair sticky on her forehead. "You made such a nice tray, too, Karen. I'm sorry." It was odd, but Tobi always got really sweet when she was sick.

The next day Karen's mother came down with the flu, or whatever it was Tobi had, and the day after, Liz got it. The main symptoms were fever, some nausea, and weakness. Karen's father put on a blue face mask, and he and Karen ran up and down stairs with trays and magazines and boxes of tissues. The little portable tv they never used anymore came out of the attic for Tobi, the one from the living room for Liz. Her mother had a stack of books on the bed with her. "Catch up on my reading," she said, her arms limp on the covers.

"Did you call into work for me again?" Liz asked the second or third morning she was sick.

"Yes, I spoke to your boss. Lori? She said just call her when you're better."

Liz blew her nose on a crumpled tissue. Her eyes were glazed, heavy-lidded. "Scott says you were at the house last week . . . and he showed you the dogs."

So it wasn't their secret anymore. Karen snapped dead leaves off Liz's pet plant. Of course she hadn't really expected him not to tell Liz. Harold and Alfred weren't exactly the kind of secret you could shove into the back of a closet. Besides, who had said anything about keeping them a secret? *Liz doesn't know yet. . . . I won't tell her.* Notice the word *yet.* Scott had been excited, joking, playing around, playing up to Karen, pleasing her, teasing her. None of it had meant anything. Not to him.

"Those dogs are going to be monsters," Liz said. "Did you see the size of their paws?" She sounded ready to weep. If Tobi got sweet when sick, Liz regressed. "I wish I wasn't sick," she whined.

"You'll feel better," Karen said, patting Liz's head. She was just about out of sympathy for sick people.

"You're hurting my head," Liz whined again. "Watch out, you'll get all my germs."

"Not me," Karen said with some satisfaction. "The last time everyone was sick, I was the only one who missed."

That day in school she sat with Marisa in assembly. "Where's Davey?"

"Karen, we're not together every minute." Marisa nudged her. "How is your love life?"

Ouch! What a question from Marisa. What was she to say? *It's great! Fabulous! Enviable!* Barefaced lies. But maybe better than the boo-hoo truth — What love life? No love life! "It's picking up."

Marisa brightened. "Yes? Is there someone —?"

Karen smiled mysteriously, as if to say, of course there's someone.

Marisa hugged her arm. "Now I'll tell you. Even though I didn't break you and Davey up, I've felt guilty. Yes, I really have. Who is he, Karen?"

She looked around the auditorium. Did she have to say the someone was Scott, to whom Liz was engaged to be engaged? "I don't see him right now." Did she have to say that there was no hope, no hope, none at all? Did she have to say that after engaged to be engaged came engaged? And after that, marriage. At which time Scott would become her brother-in-law. Her brother. In. Law. Her sibling by marriage. Liz's marriage.

She and her father ate supper alone again that night. Karen had stuck a frozen pizza in the oven, opened a can of peaches and a box of cookies. "Kiddie food," her father said, but he ate it.

They were cleaning up when the phone rang. It was Scott. "Karen?" he said on a sneeze. "Hi, hon."

"For me?" her father asked.

She shook her head.

142

"Is Liz near a phone?"

She hesitated just for a moment. "She's sleeping now, Scott."

"Oh, well, don't wake her." His voice was thick. "I just wanted to talk. I caught her flu."

"You did?" Dope. He just told you that.

"Yeah. I came home from work feeling rotten. I mean I felt rotten all day." He sounded almost as weepy as Liz.

Her father went out. Karen pushed the kitchen door closed behind him.

"Scott, do you have a fever? Are you nauseous?" Nurse Karen.

"No. Just feel rotten all over."

"Well, who's taking care of you?"

"Harold and Alfred," he said sadly. "Oh, well, I'll be all right."

After she hung up, she finished cleaning the kitchen. Poor Scott. Nobody to take care of him.

She could. She could make him custard, bring him tea, tissues, and the tv. Sick people needed help.

Karen, you're a godsend. You always know just the right thing to do.

No, it's nothing special. . . .

Don't be modest! You have a real touch with sick people. Liz — well, she's wonderful, we all know that, but when it comes to this sort of thing, she's not in the race at all.

She'd walk Alfred and Harold, feed them, straighten up the apartment. Scott would be in bed, of course. She'd sit down near him and they'd talk or, if he was feeling really awful, she'd read to him. Or maybe they'd only sit quietly, not saying anything. Just being together.

143

Above her she heard muffled thumps, somebody moving around, water in the pipes, the sound of the tv. Poor Scott! Alone in that apartment. At least her mother and her sisters were being sick together. She swept the dirt into a pile and got the dustpan.

Twenty-three

On the Oak Street bus, Karen virtuously read a short story for English. She took notes for the oral report. More virtue. She needed all the virtue she could get her hands on. Was that true? Was she doing something wrong? Was it really so terrible that she was on her way to Scott's house? What if Florence Nightingale had felt this way? Think of all the soldiers who would never have known her tender touch. Think of all the nurses who would never have been inspired to help the sick and feeble and ailing folk of the world.

Karen Florence Nightingale. On her way to cool the fevered brow and comfort the sick.

Why hadn't she told Liz her plan? That was the guilty part.

Plan? What plan? Last night, after Scott's phone call, she had imagined doing this, true. But that was fantasy, not the real stuff. If she had to tell Liz everything that went on in her mind, there'd be a revolution and she'd be up against the wall, traitor.

"Want to come over to my house and study?" Marisa had asked as they left school. And Karen had said, No, not today, she had something to do. But she only knew what it was she "had" to do, at the moment she said it. So she couldn't possibly have told Liz beforehand. But, somehow, she still felt guilty.

Look, Liz, Scott's sick and has no one to do anything for him. You should approve my giving him a bit of help, since you're feeling too zapped yourself to do anything. And, besides, Scott's also my friend, so what if I just happen to want to see him? Do I have to report in to you?

Karen Clarence Darrow, famous lawyer, arguing her case before the Supreme Court of Sisters. One moment persuasive, the next cajoling, but always with iron logic. And so your honor. . . . Say no more, Counselor. Charges dismissed!

She strolled down Oak, knapsack over her shoulder, easy and casual. A person on her way to see a friend. But at Scott's house, she lost heart. Just barge in on him? What if he hated company when he was sick? Karen, Harold, and Alfred, three big slobbering dogs falling all over Scott. Do you love me? Do you love me? Pant, pant, pant.

She sat down on the top step and argued with herself. Either go in there and see Scott, or go home. She got up, then sat down again.

Come on, someone seemed to be saying to her. *Aren't you tired of watching things happen to other people? To Tobi, Liz, Marisa . . . to everyone except you?*

She went up the stairs resolutely, two at a time. Then, on the landing, she thought if she went away now, nobody would ever know she'd been here. No up against the wall, traitor. No Florence Nightingale. No guilt. No *nothing*.

She knocked. From inside, Scott called, "Come in."

She opened the door, peeked in. "It's me."

"Karen." Scott's voice cracked. "What are you doing all the way over here?" He was unshaven, wearing unlaced work boots, pajamas, and a Snoopy sweat shirt under a bathrobe. He looked like the man with the headache in the aspirin ad. Correction. He made the man with the headache in the aspirin ad look like Mr. Vitality.

"I came to help you. You said you didn't have anybody to take care of you. Well . . . here I am."

"Really? Is that why you came?" She took off her knapsack.

"Sure."

"Your sister will kill me if you pick up my germs."

"I won't. I'm healthy as a horse. But you look awful. You should be in bed."

"I was."

"In your work boots?"

He looked down at his feet in surprise. "Oh, right. I was thinking about taking Harold and Alfred out for a walk." Hearing their names, the dogs got up, grinning, their ears laid back.

"You don't look as if you have the energy to take yourself down the stairs," she said.

"That's true." His eyes were bloodshot, his bathrobe pockets bulging with tissues. "I should get in bed, I suppose," he said vaguely, but he didn't move.

"Scott, if you want me to, I'll take the dogs out. Where are their leashes?"

147

He thought about it in slow time. "I guess we could just put them out in the backyard," he said finally. "It's fenced."

"Okay. You want me to do that?"

After another long conference with himself, he nodded. "Door through the kitchen."

The dogs romped behind her, knocking into each other. She led them out to the back porch. A flight of covered wooden steps went down into the yard. "There you go, boys, have fun." They galloped down the stairs like a cavalry charge.

Scott was still slumped on the couch when she came back. "Is that your bedroom?" She looked into the room off the kitchen. The bedding was crumpled on the floor. "I'll change the sheets, Scott. Where do you keep —"

"Ah, no, Karen —" He half rose. "I can't let you do that."

"Yes, you can. What do you think I've been doing all week for everybody at home?" Moving back and forth with the clean sheets, she said, "Have you eaten anything today?"

"I always eat." He sat down while she finished, then got in bed. All at once, after all the hustle and bustle, there was a big silence.

"Will that fence really keep the dogs in?" she asked, just to have something to say.

"It has so far." Scott's lids trembled and closed. He started snoring. When he opened his eyes he looked surprised to see her still there.

"Want some tea?" she said.

He shook his head.

"I could shave you," she offered.

He put his hand to his chin. "No," he said after a moment. "I don't mind."

She looked around the room. There was a drawing board in one corner, a bureau, a chair with some clothes draped over it and one thing that surprised her, a full-length oval mirror in a wooden frame. What now? she thought. Was that all? Was that it? Did she have to leave?

But then Scott said, "Do you play checkers?"

"Checkers?"

"Don't you like them?" He sounded disappointed. The nap had made him feel better, he said, put him in exactly the right mood for a good game of checkers.

"I usually play chess with Tobi." She got the board and checkers from the closet. Scott patted the side of his bed and after just a tiny moment she sat down. "You want red or black?"

"Red," he said. "I always play red."

After a few moves she could tell that, even sick, he was a lot more serious and a whole lot better at checkers than she was. He studied the board, frowning, tapping his lips. Was that where Liz had picked up that habit? Karen made her moves fast and without a lot of thought. It was like playing chess with Tobi. After the first few moves, she knew he was going to wipe her out.

"Not a bad game," he said, after he'd finished her off. He had crowned every one of his kings and taken almost all of hers.

"It was a terrible game. Don't laugh." She knocked the pieces onto the floor. "I'm a sore loser."

He started coughing, his face got red, and he

leaned back against the pillow. "In high school we had a checkers club. Not a chess club. That was for the brains. I was our star checkers player."

"A fine time to tell me."

"You're impressed? I never once, not in my entire checkers career, impressed a girl with that news." He reached for a cigarette from the pack on the bedside table.

"You shouldn't," she said, and held out her hand for one for herself.

"You're right. Neither should you."

"If you don't smoke, I won't."

"I'm not going to inhale," he said.

"Okay, I won't either." She stuck the cigarette between her lips.

"What are you going to do when you graduate high school?" he asked.

"I'm not totally sure yet. I have a lot of different ideas."

"That's good. I didn't know for quite a while what I was going to do. I didn't know all the way through college. Then it came to me — I've been wasting my time! All I want to do is build. . . . So, that's what I'm doing." He sat up, raising his knees. His hair was damp, curling down onto his forehead and over his ears. "What kinds of things are you interested in? What do you think about?"

"A lot of things." She looked down at the blanket, smiling a little.

"You think about the world situation?"

"Sure, don't you? Doesn't everybody?"

"Well, what do you think?"

"Bad. Very bad."

"How about the economy?"

"Gives me a headache."

"My feeling exactly. How about boys?"

"Hmmm . . . not like girls."

"Remarkable. Tell me, Karen, are kids still getting together in the same old way?"

She waved the cigarette as if to say, if he was talking about sex, nothing had changed.

"Ahh, so."

"Human nature," she said.

"You get sex ed. in school these days, don't you?"

"Not really. Family Life. I had to care for a goldfish for a week." She explained about Gladys Goldfish and Eggbert.

"I missed out on all that fun." Then he started talking about how kids really learn about sex. "I suppose you learn the most from your parents. And after that, you learn from your friends and on the street. It's not so bad."

"Maybe," she said. "And sometimes it's awful."

"What do you mean?"

"I was just thinking . . . after I started kindergarten, one of the big boys pushed me down in the playground, fell right down on top of me."

"He fell down?"

"No, he threw himself down on me, wouldn't let me get up."

She stopped, remembering how the boy had said, I fick fick fick you! Even though she'd never heard the real word, she still knew what it meant. In some way she knew and she was terrified.

"Baby rape," Scott said. "What did you do?"

She shrugged. The conversation was making her uncomfortable now. "I yelled and scared him off."

"Good for you." He lay back against the pillow

151

and a moment later, he'd dropped off to sleep again. Karen tiptoed out of the room. In the kitchen, she ate an apple and some cheese. Harold and Alfred were whining and pawing at the door. Let us in, Karen, pul-eeeeze!

"Okay, you guys, but you gotta be quiet." They tumbled in, grinning. She filled their water bowls. They sounded like Niagara Falls when they drank. "Shhh! Scott's sleeping."

When she went back into the bedroom, Scott was still asleep, lying on his side, one hand under his chin. She sat down in the chair across from the bed. The other night she and Tobi had watched a movie about a teenage girl in love with an older man. The girl, who was seventeen and incredibly sexy (Tobi disgustedly said that in real life the actress was thirty-one), went all out to make the older man see that he should let go and fall in love with her, too. Actually, secretly, he already was crazy about her, but he didn't want to admit it because he thought the difference in their ages was too great.

The girl, though, thought love was the most important thing. She didn't care about anything else! She wanted him and did just about anything she could think of to influence him, including stripping off her clothes on the beach when he was watching. He had a wife, which was the bad news, but the good news for the girl was that she didn't have to think about his wife because (luckily — or anyway, conveniently) she was someplace else, far away.

That definitely helped. Liz, for instance, was right here. What if her flu took a turn for the worse, her temperature shot up, and before they had a chance to even call the ambulance, she went into a coma?

DOA. First the shocking phone call from the emergency room doctor. *Ms. Freed? I want you to break this news gently to your mother. I have bad, very bad news....* Then the funeral, all of them weeping. Poor Scott! He'd be inconsolable. Karen would be the only one who could make the tiniest dent in his misery.

On the other hand, it would be better all around if Liz didn't die. She didn't want Liz dead. Just away. Far away. Very far away, and not coming back. For instance, if Liz were in California . . . but that wouldn't work. Liz didn't like California. Last year she'd gone out there with a girl friend for a couple weeks and come back saying she wouldn't care if the San Andreas fault opened up wide enough to swallow the whole goofy state.

Maybe she'd like to go to Africa on a safari. No, that would only be for a month at most, and then she'd be home again. Karen pondered. Since Liz didn't like the Sunshine State, maybe she'd flip for snowy Alaska. She could live in a cabin and write poems about cold and frost and polar bears. She'd be away, but happy, while Scott would be here and lonely.

Karen got up quietly so as not to wake him and looked at herself for a while in the mirror. The dogs came in. "Shhh!" Harold lay down on the floor with his chin on his paws. Alfred took over the chair, turning around and around like a cat until he got comfortable. "Thanks a lot, Alfie," Karen whispered. "Where am I supposed to sit?"

Alfred looked at her out of one eye. Suit yourself, Karen, sit on the bed, just don't bother me, pul-eeeze.

She sat down carefully on the bed. The room was quiet, just the sounds of the dogs snuffling in their sleep. Everyone was sleeping but her. She yawned and leaned back, breathing quietly. Scott had turned to lie on his other side. He faced her, the blankets pulled up around his ear, his mouth slightly open. She slid down a little, then a little more, until she was lying flat on the bed next to him.

When she woke up, Scott was looking at her, his eyes sleepy. "Hu-lo," he said.

"Hu-lo." The smell of his skin came to her: fresh wood and cigarettes and cough drops. Their faces were close. She didn't know if she could bear it, if she was going to live or die. Scott touched her chin with one finger, his face came closer still, and he kissed her.

Then suddenly the dogs were on the bed, Harold and Alfred, both of them leaping on Scott and Karen, licking their faces, grinning and happy. You're kissing? We want to kiss, too. Scott sat up, his hair mussed. He didn't look at Karen. He grabbed Alfred by the ears. "These mutts!" he said. And Karen slid off the bed, stooping to pick up the checkers.

Twenty-four

Karen's grandmother came over on Sunday, after calling up to make sure no one was still sick. "No, we're all recovered," Karen's mother said on the phone. "Liz'll come for you, Mother Freed."

"Want to come with me?" Liz said to Karen, picking up the car keys.

Overnight, the weather had turned summer hot. The inside of the car was like a furnace. "Ugggh, sticky seats." Karen rolled down her window.

"I hate it when spring gets gobbled up this way," Liz said. "But I'm not complaining," she added hastily. "I'm just glad not to be sick."

Grandma was waiting in the lobby of her building. She walked leisurely toward them, her face shadowed under a large straw hat with a pink band.

"Hello, Grandma," Karen said, getting out of the front seat and into the backseat.

Her grandmother put out her cheek for Liz's kiss.

"I said, hello, Grandma," Karen repeated louder.

"I'm not deaf, Karen. Try to remember."

155

"Sorry."

"I have excellent hearing, dear."

Karen slumped lower in the seat and closed her eyes. When life was unbearable, go somewhere else. Go to Scott's house. He had kissed her. First he had looked at her. *Hel-lo.* And then he had kissed her. *Liz, I've something to talk about to you. Scott and I don't want to hurt you, it's just that we feel we have to be honest with you. . . .*

Liz, this isn't easy to say, but you must have noticed something is wrong. We can't go on deceiving you. We? Who's we? Oh, I know in your heart of hearts you know already. Scott and I. . . .

The night before, when Scott had called, Karen answered the phone. "Hi, Karen," he'd said, "is Lizzie bird there?"

"Hold on." Hi, Karen? Was that all he had to say to her?

And what was this Lizzie bird stuff? When had he started that kind of cutesy talk? Liz detested being called Lizzie. But maybe there was a method to his cuteness. Make Liz crazy by calling her names she hated. Lizzie bird, Lizzie lizard, bizzy Lizzie. Lizzie, Laaazy, louzy blouzy frowzy Lizzy. She'd throw his engaged to be engaged ring in his face. We're through. No, I won't change my mind. Get out! Good-bye!

Then he and Karen would hop in his truck, the dogs would ride in back, and all four of them would drive off together. They'd probably keep going until they got to California, where they'd eat oranges off the trees and swim in the ocean. Happy together forever.

"I suppose exams are coming, Karen? . . . Karen?"

She sat up. "Oh. Not yet, Grandma, not till the end of June. Six more weeks."

"Are you prepared?"

"I hope so."

Her grandmother looked over her shoulder. "Don't hope for things, Karen. Make them happen. Just do it."

At home on the patio, her grandmother sat upright on a deck chair, fanning herself with a Japanese fan. "It's terribly hot." Karen brought her lemonade, ice water, a peeled cold peach. "Is that what you call peeling, dear? I can't eat that skin, it's indigestible." She peeled the peach again with the fruit knife, then bit into it. Her teeth were white and strong. "I've never lost a single tooth."

Karen's mother came out on the patio. "Mother Freed, are you comfortable?"

"Terribly hot. A bit cooler here than my apartment. . . ."

"Yes . . . unseasonable. Would you like a part of the Sunday paper?"

Karen lay in the grass. Their voices came to her distantly, a soothing hum. How odd to be old like Grandma, to be half old like her mother. Sometimes she felt sick with being young, it hurt so much, but she didn't want ever to be so old that she talked about nothing but weather and the skin on peaches.

Later, it began raining. Her parents went to a concert. Tobi had been out all day. Liz was getting ready to go out with Scott. Karen went upstairs, dragged the phone into her room, turned on the radio, and called Marisa. "Hi, I'm depressed."

"I am, too. You go first."

"No, you."

"Are you sure, Karen? I can wait —"

"No, I can, too."

"I'm fighting with my parents. I want to take a job this summer. You're right, I don't know anything about work —"

"You still remember that! I shouldn't have said it."

"No, I'm glad you did. Now here's the problem. If I work, it upsets my parents' summer plans. They want to travel. If I get a job, they think they have to stay home. I told them I'm perfectly capable of taking care of myself."

"It's not easy getting a job."

"Davey says maybe he can help me."

"Good." Karen kicked her legs in time to the music. Hardly a twinge now when she heard Davey's name.

"Your turn," Marisa said.

"Oh, it's just everything. My grandmother was over today. They're all out now, except Liz, and she's going out, too."

"With that cute guy in the red truck?"

"Right. Scott."

Did Marisa pick up on something in her voice, in the way she'd hesitated over his name? "Karen, you still haven't told me who the new love of your life is."

"I know." Karen lay on her back, pedaling her legs in the air, and thought about telling Marisa. It would be good and bad. Good, because it would be a relief to tell someone what had happened. Bad, because then the memory of what had happened wouldn't be just hers.

"What does his name begin with?"

"Can't you guessss?" she said, deliberately drawing out the *s* sound. If Marisa guessed, she wouldn't deny it.

"Oh, give me a little hint, Karen."

Karen pedaled harder. And a one! and a two! and a one! and a two! and a three! . . . Good for the thigh muscles. "No, no. If I tell you anything, you'll guess." She hissed out the word.

Guess, Marisa, guess. No, never mind, I'll tell you. It's Scott. He kissed me.

"You should tell me. I'm your best friend."

I was in his apartment. On his bed.

"So you're not going to tell?"

"Oh, I might . . . one of these days."

Downstairs, the doorbell chimed.

"Karen, get it, please," Liz yelled.

"Have to go, Marisa, see you in school."

The doorbell chimed again. It was undoubtedly Scott. She didn't want to see him. Well, yes, she did, but not this way, not coming for Liz. Let Liz answer the door herself. She turned up her radio from loud to deafening.

"Karen," Liz screamed.

Her legs flopped to the floor. She lay there another moment. What was it her grandmother had said? Something about making things happen. The kiss — had she made that happen? Or had he? Or had it just happened? She went into the hall. Lightning flashed green through the little window.

"Karen!" Liz banged open the bathroom door. She had on a white summer dress, the blue sash dangling. She was barefooted, brushing her hair. "Oh, there you are. You are going. Okay."

Karen's hand drifted over the banister. Why should

159

she open the door if Scott was here to see Liz? What was she, Norman the doorman?

Make things happen. Grandma, that's like telling a Martian to make a chocolate cake. *Just do it.* How? What's the secret?

The doorbell chimed a third time. Liz rushed past her, shoeless. Her freckles stood out like stars all over her face. "You're sleepwalking tonight. Scott'll drown out there."

Karen sat down on the stairs.

"Hi, love," Liz said, below her, "come on in."

"Mmm, you look sweet." Scott, in the hall. Kiss kiss, like birds pecking. His dark, curly hair was damp. He had shaved off his sick beard. There was a bit of tissue stuck to his skin and he wore a gold necklace.

"I'll be a moment more," Liz said. She went up the stairs, past Karen, down the hall.

Karen sat still, looking down at Scott. He hadn't noticed her.

He took a pack of cigarettes out of his pocket, stuck one in his mouth, then put it back into the pack. Did he remember that Karen had taken the cigarette from his mouth, put it into her mouth? He had said, *You'll get my germs, sweetie.* She had said, *I'm not afraid.*

No, that wasn't the way it happened. She had just made that up. What if she had made up everything? What if nothing had happened, none of it? Not her visit. Not being on the bed with him. Not the kiss.

He looked up and saw her. He walked to the stairs. One foot on the bottom step, hands in his pockets. "Hi. How are you?"

"Fine." As you can see. Why do you ask? Is something wrong with your eyes?

"Well, I'm all recovered."

"Uh-huh." Thrilled to hear it.

"Harold and Alfred say hello."

"Yeah?" Bla bla bla.

"Quiet tonight, aren't you?"

"Uh-huh." I hate you, Scott.

"Cat got your tongue?"

She thought about sticking out her tongue. How childish!

"So! How are you?"

The same way I was the last time you asked me.

"Liz and I are going to a movie."

"She told me." She was almost nauseous with anger. What a stupid conversation.

Liz came running down the stairs. "Here I am. We're taking my car, aren't we?" She got her car keys from the basket, pulled on a light jacket. Scott opened the door.

"See you later, Karen." The door slammed.

She sat there for a long time, biting her fists.

The rain increased. Thunder rattled the windows. Could lightning strike through the panes? Pane. Pain. She held her stomach. Liz and Scott in the car . . . sitting close to each other. The windshield wipers frantically beating, rain tapping on the little roof. Liz had pulled over to wait out the storm . . . so cozy in the car . . . like a little house. They'd kiss. Kiss and kiss and kiss. Not one tiny, measly kiss that lasted only a single moment, but long kisses, kiss after kiss, their arms wound around each other, making love with the rain streaming down the windows.

Twenty-five

The rain streamed down Karen's neck. "Tobi, come on, Tobi," she screamed. Tobi was coming over the top of the last hill, on the heels of a tall, fat girl in tight purple shorts. Right beside Karen, her mother and Jason were screaming their heads off, too. The rain had started about halfway into the ten-mile run sponsored by the Muscular Dystrophy Association. "They're raising funds for research," Tobi had said. "Want to sponsor me? A dollar a mile."

"Muscular dystrophy? That doesn't have anything to do with speech pathology," her mother had said.

"It's a good cause," Tobi had said. "And it's about time I entered a race. I need a challenge."

"You need a challenge, sweetie, the way a frog needs a raincoat."

Tobi came in tenth in a field of one hundred fifty. "Not bad," she said later, when the four of them stopped in the Drumlins Country Club for brunch.

She was still wearing her running shorts, with a hooded sweat shirt pulled over her T-shirt. Her hair was curly from the rain, which had stopped as suddenly as it started.

"Better than not bad, toots," Jason said. "That's great. Isn't that great, Sylvia?"

"I think so, Jason." Karen's mother nodded and smiled. Everyone was nodding and smiling at everyone else — at least Jason and her mother were doing their share. When Jason smiled he showed a gold tooth, which gave him the look of a pirate. Her mother's smile struck Karen as a touch too big, a touch too sweet. She was trying, but maybe trying too hard, to show Tobi that she accepted Jason. Karen wondered who her mother was kidding. Tobi? Or herself?

"Hey, how many people could even run ten miles?" Jason said.

"At least a hundred and fifty," Karen said.

Jason snapped his fingers, laughed, pointed at her, as if she'd said something really clever.

He was on his good behavior. Being a model person. Showing that he, too, could be a nice, ordinary human being. He had held the chair out for her mother, remembered Karen's name, and said brunch was his treat and he recommended the strawberry waffles topped with whipped cream.

But the strain of being ordinary and nice must have gotten to Jason. And the strain of smiling so much and being so bland must have kicked her mother over the edge. "How old are your children, Jason?" her mother suddenly said.

"Fourteen and eleven, Sylvia." He gleamed his gold tooth at her.

163

"Fourteen and eleven," she repeated. "And the fourteen year old is the — girl?"

"Right."

Her mother looked down at her waffle, smiling bemusedly. "What does that remind me of? Oh, I know. Tobi, remember when you baby-sat for that Muselli girl? What was her name?"

"You mean Lydia Muselli?" Tobi said. "What about her?"

"Remember — it was so funny. They called you up for New Year's Eve and asked you to baby-sit? You were about fourteen then, yourself. And when you came home, you just burst into my room and said, 'Mom! I'm only two years older than Lydia and she's four inches taller than I am and twice as smart, and I was supposed to be baby-sitting her!' "

"I don't remember that," Tobi said.

The tension at the table was so thick it could have been beaten and used as a whipped cream substitute. Except, Karen thought, feeling the real stuff gurgling in her stomach, tension probably tasted like rotten eggs.

"No?" her mother said. "That's funny. We decided maybe they had wanted Liz and gotten mixed up."

"I don't remember any of that," Tobi said. "What's the point, anyway?"

Karen glanced at Jason. He was leaning back, his arms crossed over his massive chest, his eyes on her mother, his lips and the side of his nose lifted in a mocking, knowing expression.

"Just thinking about ages," her mother said. "People's ages. Just thinking," she said quietly, "that when Jason's daughter was born, you were all of four years old, Tobi. Just thinking how you and Karen used to play together and there's — what? — something over three years between you? Actually closer to four years, isn't it?"

Tobi flushed as red as the moment she had crossed the finish line.

"Tobi — Jason —" her mother said. "Have you two thought —"

"We've thought, Mom. We've thought about lots of things, surprising as it may seem to you. I thought you told me —" She seemed to become inarticulate with rage and pushed back her chair.

"Tobi —"

"You told me! You said — oh, what's the point! I can't talk to you!"

"Tobi, I'm just —"

"Nooo!" She covered her ears.

That was the moment when Karen noticed that tension smelled like rotten eggs, too.

It was Jason who smoothed things over. He walked away from the table with Tobi, his arm around her shoulder. They stood by the window that looked out on the golf course, his head bent toward hers, talking.

"Oh. Oh. Oh," Karen's mother said. She rubbed her forehead, laughed, although she looked ready to cry. "I'm stupid. Sometimes I'm stupid."

"Mom —"

"What's the matter with me, Karen?"

"I guess you're worried about Tobi."

"But I *told* myself, Don't fight her! You don't lock horns with Tobi. You've got to give her time. She'll figure things out. I'm sure she's going to see that he's too old for her. Underneath she's sensible,

I know she is, she's not self-destructive."

"I don't like him, either," Karen said.

Her mother looked up. "Honestly, I don't know what I feel about him, except he's too old. Tobi's just — she's so tender," her mother said intensely. "She acts tough, but underneath she's so tender. I'm so afraid she's going to be hurt." She started crying, then stopped, wiping her eyes quickly as Tobi and Jason came toward the table.

They sat down and somehow they all managed to make conversation until they'd finished eating.

Later on, what stayed with Karen was the thought that when Tobi wanted something, she went out and did something about it. She fought for it. She made it happen.

On the corner of Oak Street, a girl sat upright on a chair near tubs of cream and yellow daffodils. She was pale, her hair pulled sharply back behind her ears. A hand-lettered sign at her feet said DAFFYS. GIVE ONE TO SOMEONE YOU LOVE. She reminded Karen of Mary Poppins, the same narrow-eyed, critical glance. Any moment now she might rise straight up into the air, flowers in hand, casting one last, severe glance back at the mess on Earth.

Karen bought a single daffodil with an orange center. When Scott opened the door, she would hand it to him. He would ask her in. Then she'd say, *You kissed me. It meant something, I know it did.* . . .

The downstairs door was locked. She rattled the handle. The door to the other apartment sprang

166

open, and a man with a halo of scruffy white hair looked out. "He ain't home," he said, going down the porch steps. "He's working."

"Oh."

"He got a truck," the man said, stopping at the foot of the steps. "If you see the truck, he's here. If you don't see it, he ain't here."

"Yes," she said.

The man shook his head. "Dumb people," he muttered, and he went off down the street, bandy-legged, hopping like an old gnome.

Karen went around to the back of the building. The neighborhood was quiet, slumberous in the heat. In the tiny backyard, someone had planted an equally tiny garden. She went up the wooden staircase, past the first floor apartment to Scott's back porch.

The back door was also locked, but the window leading into the pantry opened on the first try. She wasn't surprised. She hitched herself up onto the sill, balanced on her belly for a moment, then wriggled through. In the kitchen, Harold and Alfred launched themselves at the pantry door, barking halfway between threat and hope. "It's me, boys." She brushed off her knees.

Hello! they barked. We knew it was you all the time. Hello, Karen!

She closed the pantry window again. "Too bad you guys couldn't open the door for me."

We would have if we could, they cried, their nails scratching fervently. When she opened the door, they jumped up on her, pawing her and kissing her face a thousand times in gratitude for her visit.

"You're welcome, think nothing of it. Now calm down." She pushed them away and tried to adopt a severe tone. "Down. Sit. Stay."

They grinned and leaped into the air. Awww, Karen, you don't mean it.

She pushed Harold's haunches down. "Now stay there." He looked at her, abashed. She kissed him. Alfred immediately lay down on the floor. See how good I'm being! Kiss me, too!

Karen took off her knapsack, put the daffodil in water, and combed her hair. She poured a glass of apple juice and drank it quickly.

The living room was dim with the shades drawn. She sat on the floor, cross-legged. When Scott returned he would find her sitting there, studying; serious, sober, a tiny smile on her face at his surprise. How did you get in? he'd say. Magic! She'd snap her fingers. No, really, how did you? Oh, I flew down the chimney. Finally, she'd relent and tell him that he ought to keep the pantry window locked. He'd look rueful at first, then he'd laugh at her ingenuity and take out his key chain and hand her a key. Come anytime you want, Karen.

The dogs lay down near her, panting. The coolness was an illusion. Waves of heat came in through an open window. She went into the kitchen and poured another glass of apple juice. All at once she had the irresistible feeling that, at that very moment, something extraordinary had happened to her, that she had taken an immense growth spurt, had grown in height, leaped up an inch, two inches, maybe three. She went into the bedroom and stared at herself in the long mirror. Slowly the wave of ecstatic power slid away. She leaned against the wall, chewing a strand of hair. From the corner of her eye, she glanced at Scott's unmade bed. There, just beyond the edge of her vision, she saw him and Liz. . . .

Twenty-six

Karen was in the kitchen, sitting on the table, the door half shut, when she heard Scott coming in. The dogs ran to meet him. She picked up a magazine, a lit cigarette between her fingers. Her props.

"Boys, behave! Harold . . . Alfred. . . ." She smiled stagily, turning the pages of the magazine. What was he doing in there? She put down the cigarette, then picked it up again. She was dying of thirst. "Okay, boys, let's go. A quick run." The thud of the door. The faint echo of feet and paws on the stairs.

She hopped off the table, drank apple juice, then rushed into his room to check herself in the mirror. Her hair was long and loose today, held at the sides with barrettes. Rapunzel, Rapunzel, let down thy golden hair, here comes the prince to climb up the beautiful ladder of hair and rescue you. Or was she Snow White, hands crossed meekly over her chest, lying in her crystal coffin, waiting for the prince to

170

give her the kiss of life? No, no, no, she wasn't lying around like a corpse, she was making things happen.

She went back into the kitchen, sat down on the edge of the table, legs crossed, like somone in a story or a play, waiting for the action to begin, for the story to unfold. Waiting to find out what would happen. He'd come in, see her, his eyes would sparkle. Karen! You're here! How wonderful. I've been thinking about you constantly. . . . He'd take her hands, kiss them, they'd dance through the rooms. . . .

She heard him returning, talking to the dogs. "I suppose you guys are hungry now?"

"Scott," she said. Oh, how dry her throat was. There was a moment's silence. "Somebody here?"

"Scott. Me."

He padded in, stocking-footed, the dogs rollicking on either side of him. He was wearing baggy stained pants, a torn work shirt with the sleeves rolled up. There was a smear of dirt on his cheek. "Well . . . Karen. What are you doing here?"

The dogs ran back and forth between them. She came to see us, Scott! She came to visit! Ain't it great!

"Quiet," Scott said.

She took the flower from the jar in the middle of the kitchen table. "This is for you."

He looked around the kitchen. Her sneakers on the floor. The empty apple juice bottle in the sink. The open cupboard door.

"I bought this from the Mary Poppins girl on the corner."

"What are you doing here?"

She slid off the table. "I came to see you." She offered him the flower again. "Isn't it beautiful? It reminded me of a poem we read in English. 'Give me just one flower, please, because more is noisy.'"

"That's pretty, Karen."

"Aren't you going to ask me how I got in?"

"How'd you get in?"

She smiled mysteriously. "Don't you want to guess?"

"No."

So cool. His voice so level, flat. A different Scott. Someone she didn't know. As if that kiss on his bed had never been, as if the dogs, leaping up on them and slurping over their faces, had washed the kiss out of existence.

She wanted to tell him, to shout in his face, You kissed me! "I came in through the pantry window."

He poured food from a bag into the dogs' dishes. "Some places that's called breaking and entering." He took a carton of yogurt out of the refrigerator.

Her scalp burned, two straight lines of fire, one on either side. "Why are you being so unfriendly? I thought we — have I done something really terrible?"

"Oh, Karen." He put down his spoon and looked at her, straight at her for the first time. "You know, you gave me kind of a shock. I'm not used to coming home and finding people sitting around my kitchen, smoking."

"And eating and reading your magazines. And drinking your apple juice. And taking off their sneakers!"

His eyes softened. "You got it."

She moved closer to him. "I dreamed about you last night. We were picking up pennies together and you saw some money underneath a grating and you said, I don't think we can get that, Karen."

She was talking fast, too fast.

"It was real money, not just pennies, something like a thousand-dollar bill. We both wanted it. You were worried that we couldn't reach it, but I kept saying, No, no, it's a piece of cake, Scott! I was faking you out. I actually didn't have the vaguest idea how we could get it."

He leaned on his hand. "Is that why you came over, to tell me your dream?"

"Dreams are important. Did you ever dream about me?"

"No," he said, but she knew he was lying.

"You know what dreaming about someone means, don't you?"

He scraped the bottom of the yogurt container. "I didn't know it meant anything." His voice was as empty as the yogurt carton, air surrounded by plastic, the kind of voice you might use for a stranger. "Well, I have things to do." He left the kitchen.

In a few minutes she heard the shower. She put on her sneakers, washed out the juice glass. *I'm not used to finding people in my home. . . . Some places that's called breaking and entering. . . .* Cold, sarcastic stinker! Turning the charm on and off, like hot and cold taps. In a rage she sponged off the table, closed the magazine, jammed the empty apple juice jar into the garbage pail. There! Her foul, unwelcome presence was wiped out. She picked up her knapsack. "I'm going!"

173

The bathroom door opened; Scott came out in a cloud of steam. He'd changed from his work clothes into clean, pressed pants.

"I'm going now."

"Okay." He walked with her into the living room, opened the door for her, waited for her to leave.

She walked past him, her eyes filling. What had made him change? Where was the Scott who'd driven her around to look for jobs? Who'd hugged her and joked with her? Who'd talked about the future so reassuringly and played checkers like a demon? And kissed her. Yes, kissed her. Kissed her on the mouth.

"I thought we were friends. You act like you hate me!" It was horrible. She didn't want to cry and she couldn't stop.

"Karen, come on. Don't do that." He put his arm around her. "Don't . . . come on, wipe your eyes. Do you have a tissue?"

She tore away from him, wiped her face fiercely with the back of her hand. She wanted him to kiss her again, wanted it so badly. "Oh, why don't you —" She stopped, lips pressed together. Her eyes kept leaking. "I want," she began. "I want . . . I want. . . ." She held out her arms. "Kiss me. Will you kiss me?"

He leaned away from her with a pained little smile. "Karen. Oh, now — Karen, you really can't do this."

"Please."

She was so ashamed! Yet she was ready to beg him again. Please! Please! Please! He leaned toward her, looking — oh, she didn't know what to call it! Sad. Sad. . . . She couldn't think about it, couldn't think about anything. His lips touched hers. She stood absolutely still. His lips on hers. His hand touching her face. Her eyelids swelling.

The phone rang, sharp, shrill. She opened her eyes, looked straight into his eyes.

Then he went into the kitchen. "Hello? Yah, I know . . . sorry . . . I just got held up a bit. . . ."

She sat down on the floor in a stupor, her back against the couch. She heard him moving around. After a while he came back into the living room. "You're still here?" The coldness again. The remote eyes. Scott, the trapeze artist. Whooooosh! He's here. Whooooosh! He's gone. Now you see him. Now you don't.

"Yes. . . ." She could hardly hear herself. "Still here."

"I have to go out now."

"Okay."

"Which means you have to go."

She stood up clumsily, hoisted her knapsack to her shoulder, then sat down again. Where was she going? Home? She didn't want to go home. She didn't want to see Liz. Not now, after this. No, she couldn't, just couldn't. "Not yet," she said.

"What?"

"I don't want to leave yet."

"I don't understand —"

She watched his feet. He was wearing moccasins with neatly tied laces. Had he just polished his shoes? She watched his feet walk to the window, then back to her. His feet next to her feet. "All right." His voice above her. "You can stay here for a while."

God hath spoke. Thank you. Thank you, God. His shoes gleamed reddish in the light.

"Lock up when you go out."

His feet walked to the door, then back to her. His gleaming shoes shone on her. "Turn that inside lock. Will you do that?"

"Yes. Thank you." Thank you? Thank you, Scott? For what? For kissing her? For confusing her? For acting at one moment as if she were his enemy, the next as if he loved her? And then as if he could hardly wait to see the last of her!

He put his hand on her head. "Karen —" She looked up. Her eyes filled again. He seemed about to say something else, then he picked up his jacket from a chair and left.

Twenty-seven

Karen dragged her knapsack out onto the landing. She leaned against the wall, looking down the stairs, vaguely thinking about locking the door. In the living room, the dogs scratched the door. Come on baaack, Karen. It seemed ages ago that she'd bought the daffodil; it had been another time, a different dimension. And she'd been another person — positive, energetic, a person who was going to make things happen.

What if she went home and they looked at her face and knew something was wrong? Her mother could do that. So could Tobi. What if Scott was telling Liz the whole thing right now? Do you believe this, your sister climbed in my window. Look, you've got to keep that goofy kid in line. . . .

Her teeth ached and the bones over her eyes ached. She went back inside. Alfred and Harold chased around, excited to have her returned to them. Don't you want to play, Karen? Alfred put his paws on her chest. He must have seen something in her eyes; he backed off, whining.

She went into the kitchen and dialed home. Tobi answered. "I'm not coming home for supper," Karen said.

"Where are you?"

"Marisa's."

"Okay, I'll tell Mom. See you later."

"Wait a second, Tobes —" She put her hand over the receiver. Here she was at Marisa's. Here was Marisa talking to her. Want to stay overnight, Karen? Sure, Marisa. "Tobi? Tell Mom I'm staying overnight."

"Okay. See you tomorrow."

She hung up, breathing rapidly. Why had she done that? Where was she going to sleep? On the sidewalk? In a doorway?

She drank a glass of water, standing by the kitchen window, looking out, looking down into the backyard. A picture formed in her mind. Their backyard . . . a warm, windy evening . . . Liz and Scott, lying on the grass, arms around each other. . . . She rapped her forehead against the window. "Oh . . . oh . . . oh!"

Then she couldn't stand still and walked rapidly around the apartment, in and out of every room, looking at everything, touching everything — Scott's records, a screwdriver, books, an opened pack of cigarettes, a little silver bell, the towels jumbled in the bathroom.

She thought she was losing her mind.

She was in his bedroom. She paced back and forth, touched the chair, the desk, passed herself in the pier mirror. She opened a bureau drawer, a

178

college pennant fell out. Suddenly she pulled off her jeans and shirt, dropped them on the floor, and put on Scott's pajama bottoms and a T-shirt.

She was losing her mind. She sat down at his desk and started writing very fast, scribbling in a huge scrawl on both sides of a sheet of paper, almost no punctuation, just the words rushing out.

"Dear Scott I don't know what you think of me, because you acted so strange toward me today but I know just how I feel about you I love you I have loved you for a long time no not from the very beginning when you and Liz first started going together I just liked you a lot then and I liked you more every time you came to the house — then I started to love you I mean love the real stuff Im not kidding about this — dont know exactly when it happened I mean dont know the very instant and anyway I didn't mean it to happen — nobody plans stuff like that it would be like planning a tornado or a flash flood — and something else, I didn't think I'd ever tell you or be writing a letter like this no — I didn't hope for anything how could I, how could I compete with Liz — couldn't couldn't couldn't, then I began to think hope believe hope hope hope hope that something was happening maybe you felt something for me too then I came to see you when you were sick and you know what happened then, Scott, it wasn't just me —"

She dropped the pen and crumpled the paper. She started crying again and threw herself down on his bed.

Twenty-eight

She must have fallen asleep; it was dark when she woke up, her eyes were sore, her face stiff from crying, and she was hungry. Even in the darkness, she knew where she was and how she got there. She knew instantly. She was in Scott's apartment, in his bedroom, on his bed. She had gone crazy, but she was sane now.

She turned over and looked at the little glowing red face of the clock. She had slept for hours, as if dead.

I'm staying over at Marisa's. Excellent. And now what? She tried to think. Scott coming back . . . finding her still here. No. Had to leave. Go someplace. Where? She fumbled for the light — and heard someone laugh.

Her hand on the switch. Mouth open like a fish. Then that ripple of laughter again, a dim, underwater sound. She slid off the bed, heavy, slow, like moving through water. Heard the murmur of voices . . . the clicking of the dogs' paws. One voice, clearly

180

Scott's. And the other, lighter, softer, chillingly familiar.

"I admit, it was fun." That was Scott.

Light seeped under the door. They were in the kitchen.

"I had a feeling you'd like it." That was Liz.

Karen sank down on the floor, drowning, hardly able to breathe. Liz, here, in Scott's kitchen, the only thing between her and her sister a door that suddenly seemed as flimsy as seaweed.

"Can't blame me for wondering what we were in for," Scott said. "A puppet show —"

"But, sweetie, when you went up on stage — oh, that was beautiful, really beautiful."

Karen opened and closed her mouth. *Hello, out there, you're not alone. There's an intruder fish in your pond, a listener, a silent fish, a foreign fish.*

"I was amazed when you did that," Liz said. "I wouldn't have the nerve. And the way you were — as if that puppet were real —"

"Tell you the truth, I forgot that he wasn't."

"You were so serious about it all —"

Her head floated. If she whispered Liz's name — is that the way fish did it? *Glurp glurp bubble blurp —* Liz, in fish talk. Liz would say, *What's that?* She'd open the door, discover Karen swimming around on the floor in Scott's pajamas.

And what would Liz say then? *What does this mean, Karen? Scott, why is my sister in your house?*

I don't know anything about this, Liz!

That's true, Liz, noble Karen would say. *Liz, it was my idea, not Scott's.*

"I didn't make a fool of myself?" Scott said.

"No, love. I just fell for you all over again."

181

A little laugh, a murmur, an almost silence. The almost silence of two people kissing.

The hell with nobility. What if, right now, she opened the door, walked into the kitchen. *Hello, Liz.* Calm, self-possessed Karen. Or maybe she'd say nothing, drink a glass of water, light a cigarette. And let Liz think anything she wanted to think.

The silence broke. Little noises of chairs scraping, the refrigerator being opened and shut. They were talking . . . something about a trip, maps. . . . Suddenly the bedroom door opened, light poured in. "It's in here somewhere," Scott was saying. "Hold on a moment —" Then he saw Karen.

And behind him, Liz said, "Do you want me to come help you look for it?"

"No, Liz. No, don't bother." He closed the door. A furious smile passed over his face. "Oh, hell!" he whispered. "What are you doing here?"

"I stayed." She didn't know what else to say.

"I see you did!"

In the kitchen, she heard Liz singing. " . . . oh, there was no way I'd come your way. . . ."

Karen had never had anybody look at her like that. It was frightening. "Scott —"

"Quiet!" He clamped his hand over her mouth, pressed down on her head as if he wanted to push her through the floor, sink her, drown her, make her disappear.

"Mmrrrghh!" She pushed his hand off her mouth.

"Are you going to do anything crazy?" he whispered.

"No!"

He kept looking at her, as if trying to decide if he could believe her. "Now listen to me. I'm going to get Liz out of here. You stay right here."

"Why?"

He stared at her. "Why? Are you totally out of it, Karen?"

"Why do I have to stay here?" she whispered fiercely.

"Because I say so!"

"Scott?" Liz called.

"Coming, sweetie." He flicked off the light and went out, closing the door hard behind him.

"Find it okay?" Liz asked.

"No. Listen, Liz — I just developed a really weird headache, it hit me just like that, right across the back of my head."

"Oh, I'm sorry. Let me massage your neck, maybe that'll help."

Their voices faded. Karen sat on the bed, unmoving. Now they were in the living room. Murmuring. Then silence. Kissing? Do you make love when you have a headache? Do you make love when someone else is in the apartment? The clock ticked, *tick tick tick tickticktickticktickticktick*. . . . After a long time, she heard the front door closing.

Twenty-nine

Alfred scratched at the door, whimpering as if he knew that Karen was sitting in the dark. Karen . . . Karen . . . do you need rescuing? Here I am. Here comes the rescuer! She opened the door and he romped in. Remembering his errand of mercy, he braked hard and sat down in front of her, his eyes sympathetic but his ears perked for fun. St. Jokey with his jug of wine — could he help it if, in spite of her misery, he was still enjoying life? She hugged him and cried a little into his neck.

When Alfred decided she'd had enough comforting, he lay down with his head tucked under one of his huge baby paws and snoozed off. "Alfred, no! Don't go to sleep now, don't leave me." One eye opened. Sorry, Karen, you're on your own.

She pushed at her cheeks, drew in, and held a long, shuddery breath. Stop it. Stop crying. No more. Enough! She wiped her nose with the back of her hand like a little kid. The gesture angered her. Don't move, Scott had ordered, as if she were five years old. Stay right there until I come back. What did he think she would do? What terrible, horrible, unimaginable, depraved acts did he think she would commit?

Was she going to be obediently sitting here when he returned? In the same place, in the same wet, choking mood? And still wearing his pajamas. His pajamas! The visible sign of her passion, her obsession, her craziness, her nutty, unreal belief that he was in love with her.

She pulled on her jeans, fumbled with the buttons on her shirt. The faster she moved, the greater the sense of urgency. She ran her hands quickly over the bed, straightening and smoothing, hung up the pajamas, gathered the damp tissues she'd dropped on the floor. Had she forgotten anything? Her knapsack. She picked it up, stuck her feet into her sneakers, and left the room.

In the kitchen, Harold was asleep under a chair. The table was littered with the remains of Liz's and Scott's snack. Bowls, nutshells, a limp ice-cream carton dripping the sticky cream onto the table. Why was she so hungry? It seemed indecent to be miserable and hungry at the same time, as if her stomach had no respect for the pain of her feelings.

She opened the refrigerator and crammed tuna fish into her mouth. When Scott came back, she'd be gone. His kingdom, his castle, would be all his again. The mad, watery witch banished. The prince spared the nasty job of throwing her into the moat to drown. She'd salvage a little something from this wreck, a tiny scrap of her dignity. She'd leave on her own. Maybe it was diving deep and coming up with nothing but a handful of pebbles to call that

185

a dignified exit, but at the moment it was the best she could do.

She was in the hall, the door closed and locked behind her, before she slowed down enough to ask herself where, exactly, she was going. It was well past midnight. No buses. Walk across the city at this hour? Not too smart. Even if she did and got home safely, what would she say to her parents? How explain creeping in, in the small hours of the morning? Well, I know you thought I was at Marisa's, but. . . . You weren't at Marisa's? Actually, no. . . . Then where were you? I really can't say. . . .

She sat down on the steps, her head in her hands. Think, Karen. You haven't been doing too well in that department, but try. Odd thoughts and scenes passed through her mind, as if she were dreaming or half awake. Faces came and went. The Mary Poppins girl . . . the little gnome who lived downstairs . . . Mr. Radosh, the principal . . . and Rachel in her father's office. . . . Then she heard someone say, *Voices from the other world.* What other world? Where? Was there a map showing the way? *I want to go there. How do I get in? Someone tell me!* Should she just knock on the door and say, *Is this the other world?*

Then Scott was standing in front of her. She looked at him dazedly. What was he doing here? He stood away from her, hands jammed in pockets, as if she were a contagious disease.

"I'm going home," she said.

"Good. Do you want to say anything to me?"

"Like what?" she whispered.

"You're the inventive one. I'm sure you have something to say to me."

She shook her head.

"Okay, let's go. I'll drive you. You figure out what you're going to tell your folks. *Not* that you were here. That's understood, isn't it?"

She swallowed the soreness in her throat. "I can't go home. It's too late. I told them — I called and said I was sleeping over at my friend's."

Scott leaned back against the wall. "Ah. Of course. Sleeping over at a friend's. Congratulations. What do we do now with you?"

"I'll stay out here. I can sleep right here —"

"No, you can't."

"Why not? I'll go, then." She stood up.

He grabbed her arm. "Are you really crazy? I'm not letting you out to wander around the streets in the middle of the night."

"What do you care? Leave me alone."

He unlocked the door. "You can sleep on the couch." He held the door open. "Come on." He yanked her. "Come *on!*"

She went in. He threw a blanket and a pillow down on the couch. She lay down with her clothes on. She heard him moving around the kitchen, the water running, Harold snoring. The kitchen light went out. She found an apple in her knapsack, ate it, chewing the seeds; they were full of arsenic or something like that, maybe she'd be dead by morning. She pulled the blanket over her shoulders.

In the morning, she woke up early and went, in her stocking feet, into the bathroom. She was at the sink when she remembered the letter she'd written

Scott. What had she done with it? Her heart sank. The desk. She'd left it on Scott's desk.

Scott was sleeping, the blankets pulled up over his head, Alfred at the foot of the bed. The room was dim. She crept across the room, fumbled over the desk. Nothing. No letter. Her breathing sounded loud enough to wake the neighbors. She emptied the wastebasket on the floor, pushed aside scraps of paper and orange peels, found her letter crumpled up. Had she thrown it away? Or had he found it and read it?

"Karen?" Scott pushed himself up in the bed. "Karen? What are you doing, Karen?"

"I left something here — it's nothing, a letter, a letter I wrote you." She shouldn't have said it! She stood there, looking at him. She noticed the way the hair grew on his chest in a dark, thick line between his nipples. "Scott. . . ."

"Kaaren," he mimicked. But he was different this morning, not so angry, his eyes brown again, not that muddy black. He yawned and almost — could she believe it? — smiled.

And then she did something nutty again. She dropped to her hands and knees, his third dog, and crawled to the bed. He looked at her in astonishment. She reached for his hand, held it beseechingly. "Scott, I'm sorry, sorry about everything!" She kissed his hand. "Do you forgive me?"

"Karen, cut it out! Stand up, for God's sake."

She crawled onto the bed, flung her arms around him, smelled his skin. "I only did it because I love you."

"You know you're really crazy." He rumpled her hair, the way he would rumple Alfred or Harold.

He was smiling at her, he didn't hate her anymore. He held her tighter, she closed her eyes, he was going to kiss her, she knew he was going to kiss her, all the love came flooding back, and he did kiss her.

Then it was over. He pushed her away, pushed her hard, pushed her right off the bed. "Damn it, Karen!" She looked at him dazedly. "Damn it," he said again, "damn it, damn it, stay away from me, damn it!" He wrapped the covers around himself and leaped out of the bed, trailing sheets, skinny legs and bare feet showing. She wanted to laugh. Wasn't laughter healing? Laugh, Karen! Right now, right this minute, she needed to laugh! Her lips trembled, and she walked out.

She ate breakfast in a diner that morning, greasy eggs, and toast with too much butter, and coffee that she liked a lot. She drank it hot, with plenty of cream, and asked for another cup. She went into the bathroom and stood in one of the booths, crying again. She washed her face in front of the spotted mirror and, remembering how crazy she had acted, she felt an odd mixture of shame and pride. In school, she saw Marisa and Davey in the corridor; they seemed so innocent, so sweet together.

It wasn't until that night, when she was undressing for bed, that she discovered she was still wearing Scott's T-shirt underneath her shirt. She shoved it in the back of her closet with the other T-shirt, the one she'd taken from Liz.

Thirty

O ver the long Memorial Day weekend, the Freed family drove up to Piseco Lake in the Adirondacks where they had rented a house. It sat up on a little hill above the lake, a stand of birches on one side, on the other a cottage with a wooden sign over the door, GOOD VIEWS.

Blossom and Daisy Steeber, who owned the rambling, drafty house, lived up behind the hill in a cozy, overheated cottage with low ceilings. Blossy and Dase, as they were known, were both large women, tall and fat, with glasses and enormous, pillowy bosoms. Blossy was the outdoor person, fixing anything that went wrong anywhere on the property, while Dase hardly ever stuck her face out of the house, even on the hottest summer day. Blossy had a son, William, who sometimes showed up to give a hand to his mother and his aunt.

It was something of a Freed family tradition to rent the lake house for long holiday weekends. They had been doing it ever since Karen could remember.

One or the other of the sisters nearly always brought along a friend, sometimes friends. They'd all share the dormitory bedroom upstairs — five cots, five wobbly bureaus — hang around in the mornings giggling in their sleeping bags, eat like pigs, play cards for pennies, and visit Dase and Blossy at the cottage so they could gobble Dase's ginger cookies.

Karen asked Marisa to come to the lake, but she'd already made plans with Davey for a bicycle trip. "My parents are having fits, but if they're not going to let me stay home and work this summer, they've got to let me do something! That's all there is to it," she said, but a moment later, pressing Karen's arm, she asked anxiously, "Do you think I'm right?"

"Of course."

"Oh, good," Marisa said. "Thanks!"

When she heard that Liz had invited Scott for the weekend, Karen thought of staying home, but what would she say? What would be her excuse? She couldn't use Marisa this time. Then Tobi invited Jason and announced it at supper. "Him up there with us, too?" Karen's father said. He didn't look too happy. "Where are we going to put everyone?"

"Jason and Scott can share the back bedroom," her mother said. "You and I will take the screened porch. And the girls can have the dormitory, as usual."

That, Karen thought, was about the only as-usual thing about the weekend. Everything was upside-down, wrong, awful, horrible. Scott's being there was the worst part of it. She couldn't bear looking at him anymore. Even hearing his voice made her skin shiver.

At the end of May, the deep Adirondack lake was

191

too icy for swimming. Every year, someone was sure to say, "What's the matter with us? Why do we come to the lake when we can't even go swimming? We're so strange! Maybe we should find another place for next year." No one ever took it seriously; in fact, they were proud of their "strangeness."

This year, on the very first day, Jason asked the same question. "Why do you people come up here if you're not going to swim?" It was somehow different coming from him, as if he were questioning their judgments, their taste, everything that made up the Freed family lake "tradition." He put on a tight satin bikini suit, draped a towel around his neck, and went down to the dock.

Liz ran after him. "Don't be crazy! You'll have a heart attack! That water is freezing!" Jason dived in and swam a vigorous overhand crawl for about four minutes. Karen and her parents crowded out to the porch to watch. Scott stayed inside, reading a magazine. Tobi strolled down to the dock, arriving just in time to hand Jason the towel as he climbed out of the water. He danced around, pounding his chest. It wasn't clear if it was to warm himself up or a triumphal war dance.

"It was great," he said, when he came up to the house. He laughed and tousled Scott's hair. "Hey, boy, you ought to try it."

"Yeah, boy," Scott said, jerking away, "maybe I will, some other year."

Part of the tradition, part of the fun of going to the lake house had always been to spend hours outside on the big porch that wrapped around three sides of the house. They star-watched on the un-roofed side, lying flat on their backs on blankets thrown down on the floor, Dr. Freed playing teacher, a star book open on his chest, beaming a torch into the sky. "See that blue-white star, that's Vega. Now who remembers what constellation it's in?"

They had played bridge and chess on the rickety little wicker porch tables, kept an enormous puzzle going on another table — everyone who passed would stop and add a piece or two — they read and napped on the lumpy old couches, and every year her mother said, "I don't know why, but I always sleep better on this awful couch than in my own bed." The porch had been their outdoor living room, everyone's favorite place. You could even sit out there when a storm swept across the lake and watch the green lightning strikes over the water.

But this year, almost as if the weather was underlining how changed everything was, the big, dramatic lake storms were absent. Instead, day after day, fog and rain filled the air. The windows streamed, the rain pounded on the tin roof. Had the house always been this damp and creaky? They kept a fire going in the cast iron stove in the living room, but the moment you walked away from it, you felt the damp creeping in.

The morning after they arrived, Jason rapped on the dormitory door. "Tobi Freed, come out." He opened the door, stuck his enormous, gleaming head in. "Up, woman."

Tobi waved an arm at him from under her sleeping bag. "I'm coming. Scram, Jase, I'll be there when I'll be there."

But the moment he closed the door, she got up, and then so did Liz. "You sleeping in?" Liz asked Karen. She pulled on overalls, an embroidered shirt, a big knit sweater. "See you." And off she went. To be with Scott, of course.

Karen got out of bed. Did she hate Scott? She didn't know, she really didn't. Maybe she still loved him, and hated him, too. She was really clear about only one thing. She didn't want anybody to know what had happened in his apartment. Not her mother, not her father, especially not Liz.

She avoided Scott as much as possible. If he came into a room, she walked out. She never talked to him. She didn't think anybody noticed. But it wasn't always possible to avoid him. Meals were communal, and in the evening there was no other place to be comfortable except the living room.

Curled up on the couch, Karen stared into the fire, waiting for enough time to pass so she could go to bed without anyone's commenting. Her father, arm linked through hers, kibbitzed with Liz and Scott as they played checkers. Tobi flipped the pages of a ten-year-old magazine; her mother was knitting. Standing by the window, giving out one hair-raising yawn after another, Jason said abstractedly, "Nature sure is boring."

The next day was the same, except they didn't even have the distraction of Jason's swimming. It rained. Everyone hung around the house. Nothing got off the ground, nobody wanted to do any of the things they'd done other years, like making s'mores over the fire or playing trivia games or speculating about Dase and Blossy.

Liz and Scott put on slickers and rubber boots and went out for a walk, then Tobi and Jason went out, but in a different direction. Karen tried to settle down with one of the chewed-up fifties science-fiction novels that were all over the house. Her mother was curled up on the opposite end of the couch. "Mexo," Karen read, "called Linko in for consultation. 'Linko, you say you believe there are other worlds out there in the galaxy? Surely they're not as advanced as ours?' Linko clasped his six hands in front of his chest. There, at that very point, Mexo's thoughts came to him. 'Mexo,' he said soundlessly, projecting his thoughts to Mexo's —"

"Karen?" her mother said. Karen put down her book. "Are you okay, sweetie?"

Karen nodded.

"You seem — I don't know. You're so quiet lately. Has something happened?"

Karen shook her head.

"Are you sure? Do you want to talk to me?"

"I guess I'm just — just —" She wanted to say bored! Tired! Anything to fill in the gap. But her mother was looking at her so sympathetically that her throat swelled and she couldn't speak. It was awful. She couldn't take it. Not sympathy. Not now.

"It's really a shame Marisa couldn't come up," her mother said. "I know it's hard on you this year."

"I'm okay."

Her mother patted her leg. "I hate to see you feeling so down. Want to do a puzzle together?"

"No, Mom. It's okay. Really. This book is great." That brightened her mother up.

"Maybe I'll read it when you're done."

"Sure." Karen picked up the silly book again. When Liz and Scott came back a little later, she left the room. She thought she felt Scott's eyes on her, felt them almost like words. But what was he saying? He had nothing to say to her. And she had less than nothing to say to him.

But after lunch, when she was washing the dishes, Scott came into the kitchen. "Hello, Karen."

Don't say hello to me! Just leave.

He sat down on a high stool. "Want some help?"

I don't want anything from you.

"I've got good dish-drying credentials."

She held a glass up to the light, dipped it into the suds again. The back of her neck was rigid as a flagpole.

"I feel you've been avoiding me."

Really? I can't understand where you got that idea. "Karen —" He whistled through his teeth, a little questioning whistle. "I want to talk to you. Have something to say to you —" His voice so mild, hesitant. Did he think she'd forgotten how he'd cursed her? Kissed her, then cursed her. *Damn it! Damn it, get out of here!* "About that morning —" He bent closer to her. "Do you know what I'm referring to?"

She threw a handful of silver into the sink. Water splashed up.

"You seem pretty mad at me, Karen." He sighed. "Look, I've been thinking about that morning and I have to say — I should say —"

"You don't have to say anything," she burst out. "I don't want to talk about it. I don't want to hear anything you have to say."

"I can understand that —"

"Can you?"

"I don't want you to be bitter, Karen, that's partly what I want to say. I mean —"

She turned on him. "I don't care what you mean!

196

I told you, I don't want to talk about it."

"You don't want to talk about what?" Liz said.

Karen's stomach drummed. She hadn't heard the door open, nor had Scott from the look on his face.

"What's happening? You two look like you're conducting a funeral."

Scott got up, knocking over the stool. "Oh, we're just chatting. Want to go for a walk?"

"Another one? No, thanks, I'm walked out. Anyway, maybe we should help Karen clean up."

"No! I don't want any help."

Liz glanced at her, then at Scott. He picked up the stool. Then they went out. Karen finished the dishes mechanically, rinsed out the sink, and went into the living room. Her mother was sleeping outside on the porch, all wrapped up in a blanket. Her father was cleaning out his baitbox. He glanced up, smiled at her. "All done? Make sure you get one of your sisters to pull kitchen duty tonight."

She sat down again with Mexo and Linko, reading, turning pages, words entering her mind meaninglessly. *I don't want you to be bitter.* What business was it of his? Why did he even care? Let him just go away and leave her alone. She'd made a huge mistake, acted like a fool — did that mean she had to be reminded of it for the rest of her life?

Thirty-one

R eady?" her father whispered. Karen nodded.
They went quietly down the stairs. Nobody
else was up yet. Outside, the sun coming up over
the trees across the lake looked like a big, smooth,
yellow egg. Their footsteps clattered in the quiet as
they walked to the end of the T-shaped dock. "We
could take out a boat," her father said.

"No, we always fish off the dock." It was their
last day at the lake house. She wanted something,
one thing at least, to be just as it always had been.
Ever since she'd been a little girl, she and her father
would fish off the end of the dock. They baited up
and dropped their lines into the water. She caught
the first sunfish, then her father caught two pretty
little perch, and Karen caught another sunny. It was
a perfect, peaceful hour.

Even the violence of killing and cleaning the fish,
her least favorite part, was easier today, because it,
too, was a repetition of past years. They knelt down
on the dock, side by side, the fish on the stringer

g to say, damn it, I was definitely attracted to
At first I thought it was kind of cute the way
iked me, and it was fun. I wasn't hurting any-
I wasn't hurting Liz. But then —" His voice
bed. "I'm not proud of the way I acted finally.
were there that morning, it wasn't an easy
ion — okay, that's true. Right there and so
—"

line tugged her hand. A fish flapped franti-
on the hook. She pulled the hook out and
the fish back in the water.

it," he said, "don't go yet. Did you hear me?
know what I'm saying? I'm taking respon-
Karen, for that morning, for the things you

shocked her into anger. Take responsibility
t she did? It was theft. "Oh, no, you don't,"
. "Oh, no, you don't." She brushed by him
it up to the house.

afternoon, everyone scattered. The house
. Karen sat out on the porch, perched on
ng. Clouds covered the sun, uncovered it,
it. A silver light spilled across the lake.
eard voices and saw Liz and Scott below
e path. They were walking away from her,
other houses on this side of the lake. She
them. Only hours earlier, Liz had been here
e place, also watching. Karen felt her face
ke Liz's, calm, considering, watchful. No.
t Liz. She thumped off the railing, knocked
wicker table, and went inside, letting the
r slam.

upstairs, taking a nap, when Liz came
?" Liz bent over her, shaking her, her

flopping and leaping on the boards. Her father
stunned each one with a blow to the head, using
the side of the red fish scissors, and passed it to
Karen, who slit the belly and pulled out the guts,
then passed it back to her father for scraping.

When he took the fish up to the house, she decided to stay. "Maybe I'll catch a few more." She
took in two sunnies, one right after the other, both
too small. She threw them back. A motorboat raced
by, whipping up the water, a door slammed somewhere, a dog howled. She had a few more bites,
little guys, probably the same dumb fish. Sneakers
clattered on the dock, breaking into her peaceful
concentration. It was Scott, trotting toward her,
hands in the pockets of his windbreaker.

She fumbled in the tomato juice can for a worm.
Too skinny, what she and her father called a lastie.
She dropped it back, found a fat worm. Beauty! as
her father would say.

"We didn't really get to talk the other day, Karen."

Bla bla bla. Glub glub glub. What was this big,
unwelcome fish doing here?

"Something happened that we can't — I can't just
ignore." He touched her head. "Karen —"

She jerked away, jabbed the hook through the
worm.

"Look. Look, look, don't be like that." He squatted down next to her. "There are some things on
my mind. From my point of view, we need to talk."

She stood up, cast, concentrating on the line, the
little nibbles, the dazzle of the sun on the water.

He stood close to her, spoke into her ear. "I've
had this impulse to tell Liz what — to actually just
tell her and —"

She didn't believe him. He wouldn't do a crazy thing like that.

"I don't know if it's self-destructive, or what, but a couple times I've been right on the verge."

Something nibbled her worm, a rock bass for sure. She yanked in the line. Cleaned. Rockies could nibble you to death.

He leaned against the pilings, looking down into the water. "We should talk. We might not have another chance to talk alone like this."

Another worm on the hook, then the cast. Scott was like the rockies. Nibble, nibble, nibble, no stopping him, he'd nibble her to death. She yanked hard on the line.

"Karen. Will you stop fishing for two seconds and talk to me?"

"All right! Okay."

"Okay?"

"Okay! Go ahead. Talk. Go on, talk. You said you wanted to talk!"

"I do, but I want you to talk to me, too."

"I don't have anything to say."

He looked upset. Did he want her to feel sorry for him?

"I don't know," he said finally. "I thought I had it all figured out, what I wanted to say to you. I don't know, it's just — ever since that morning I've been really down on myself and feeling that I had to talk to you, explain things. And now — I'm not saying anything."

"Maybe that's the way we're talking," she said coolly. "Maybe that's it."

"You're not making this easy for me, Karen." He took her arm. That was when she saw Liz up on

the porch, looking down at t of them.

The two of them, close. Hi they were lying next to each c as the moment he'd kissed h pushed her away, pushed h pulled away from him, thre

"I'm sorry," he said. "T want to say. That's what I I I'm *sorry*, Karen."

A blurry smile swam ac smile that isn't a smile at for?" He hadn't broken hadn't written a berserk lo on his hands and knees!

"The way I acted. It v did . . . I. . . ."

She'd lived in a drear Scott, the dream of love those loony things? Cr putting on his pajamas *I love you . . . I love y* to remember! Not no had passed, a long ti she could think about

She'd fallen in love so loony? Or was it Scott, with her siste wasn't immune to I the thought that Liz of them. See, Liz! saying, I can do th that was despicabl

Scott was still ta

tryin you! you one. drop You situat sweet The cally threw "W Do yo sibility did — That for wha she saic and we That emptied the raili covered She h her on th past the watched in the san become li She wasn past the screen do She wa in. "Karei fingers digging into Karen's arm. "Wake up."

Karen sat up. Liz's face hovered over her, a round cheese, sharp cheese. Liz continued to shake her. Karen thought she might still be asleep, dreaming, mixing things up the way dreams did. Tobi would shake her, Tobi would dig into her flesh with hard fingers. Not Liz.

"Scott told me. He told me everything." Her freckles were like spots of light on her face.

"He told you?"

"That's what I said! He told me about you going to his place, he told me the whole thing. He told me everything."

"Why? Why'd he tell you?" Her toes throbbed as if someone had tramped on them, crushed them with hobnailed boots.

"I asked him. I knew something was wrong. I saw the way you two were acting. Do you think I'm utterly blind?"

Karen turned over and over in the bed.

"What did you think you were doing? Did you think at all? Did you think of anyone but yourself and your little adolescent crush? Do you know what you did? I mean, really did? You betrayed me."

Karen was shaking under the covers. She huddled into herself, knees pulled up, arms tight to her body.

Thirty-two

"K aren Freed?" the voice on the phone said.
"Yes."

"This is Kevin Mason."

"I'm sorry, we don't buy anything over the phone."

"What? Oh, you think — I'm not a salesman. This is Kevin Mason."

"Who?"

"Kevin Mason," he said loudly.

"I'm not deaf," she said, sounding like her grandmother.

"What? Is this Karen Freed?"

"Yes!"

"Well," he said patiently, "this is Kevin Mason."

"I give up. Who are you?"

"You don't remember?"

He sounded so disappointed she hurried to reassure him. "Oh, sure, I just — you know, for a moment —"

"I've got your name here," he said. "The job's open. Do you want it?"

flopping and leaping on the boards. Her father stunned each one with a blow to the head, using the side of the red fish scissors, and passed it to Karen, who slit the belly and pulled out the guts, then passed it back to her father for scraping.

When he took the fish up to the house, she decided to stay. "Maybe I'll catch a few more." She took in two sunnies, one right after the other, both too small. She threw them back. A motorboat raced by, whipping up the water, a door slammed somewhere, a dog howled. She had a few more bites, little guys, probably the same dumb fish. Sneakers clattered on the dock, breaking into her peaceful concentration. It was Scott, trotting toward her, hands in the pockets of his windbreaker.

She fumbled in the tomato juice can for a worm. Too skinny, what she and her father called a lastie. She dropped it back, found a fat worm. Beauty! as her father would say.

"We didn't really get to talk the other day, Karen."

Bla bla bla. Glub glub glub. What was this big, unwelcome fish doing here?

"Something happened that we can't — I can't just ignore." He touched her head. "Karen —"

She jerked away, jabbed the hook through the worm.

"Look. Look, look, don't be like that." He squatted down next to her. "There are some things on my mind. From my point of view, we need to talk."

She stood up, cast, concentrating on the line, the little nibbles, the dazzle of the sun on the water.

He stood close to her, spoke into her ear. "I've had this impulse to tell Liz what — to actually just tell her and —"

She didn't believe him. He wouldn't do a crazy thing like that.

"I don't know if it's self-destructive, or what, but a couple times I've been right on the verge."

Something nibbled her worm, a rock bass for sure. She yanked in the line. Cleaned. Rockies could nibble you to death.

He leaned against the pilings, looking down into the water. "We should talk. We might not have another chance to talk alone like this."

Another worm on the hook, then the cast. Scott was like the rockies. Nibble, nibble, nibble, no stopping him, he'd nibble her to death. She yanked hard on the line.

"Karen. Will you stop fishing for two seconds and talk to me?"

"All right! Okay."

"Okay?"

"Okay! Go ahead. Talk. Go on, talk. You said you wanted to talk!"

"I do, but I want you to talk to me, too."

"I don't have anything to say."

He looked upset. Did he want her to feel sorry for him?

"I don't know," he said finally. "I thought I had it all figured out, what I wanted to say to you. I don't know, it's just — ever since that morning I've been really down on myself and feeling that I had to talk to you, explain things. And now — I'm not saying anything."

"Maybe that's the way we're talking," she said coolly. "Maybe that's it."

"You're not making this easy for me, Karen." He took her arm. That was when she saw Liz up on the porch, looking down at them. Seeing the two of them.

The two of them, close. His eyes. Close as when they were lying next to each other on the bed. Close as the moment he'd kissed her. Close as when he'd pushed her away, pushed her onto the floor. She pulled away from him, threw in the line.

"I'm sorry," he said. "That's it. That's what I want to say. That's what I have to say. Have to say. I'm *sorry*, Karen."

A blurry smile swam across her face, the sort of smile that isn't a smile at all. "You're sorry? What for?" He hadn't broken into anyone's house, he hadn't written a berserk love letter, he hadn't crawled on his hands and knees!

"The way I acted. It wasn't just you. Me, I — I did . . . I. . . ."

She'd lived in a dream for weeks, the dream of Scott, the dream of love. Why else had she done all those loony things? Crawling in his window . . . putting on his pajamas . . . flinging herself on him. *I love you . . . I love you. . . .* No, she didn't want to remember! Not now. Maybe when enough time had passed, a long time, months, or even a year, she could think about it.

She'd fallen in love. Was that in itself so awful, so loony? Or was it that she'd fallen in love with Scott, with her sister's boyfriend? Even now, she wasn't immune to him, wasn't immune, either, to the thought that Liz was up there watching the two of them. See, Liz! one little part of her mind was saying, I can do the same things you can do. Oh, that was despicable. She hated herself drearily.

Scott was still talking. Would he never stop? "I'm

201

trying to say, damn it, I was definitely attracted to you! At first I thought it was kind of cute the way you liked me, and it was fun. I wasn't hurting anyone. I wasn't hurting Liz. But then —" His voice dropped. "I'm not proud of the way I acted finally. You were there that morning, it wasn't an easy situation — okay, that's true. Right there and so sweet —"

The line tugged her hand. A fish flapped frantically on the hook. She pulled the hook out and threw the fish back in the water.

"Wait," he said, "don't go yet. Did you hear me? Do you know what I'm saying? I'm taking responsibility, Karen, for that morning, for the things you did —"

That shocked her into anger. Take responsibility for what she did? It was theft. "Oh, no, you don't," she said. "Oh, no, you don't." She brushed by him and went up to the house.

That afternoon, everyone scattered. The house emptied. Karen sat out on the porch, perched on the railing. Clouds covered the sun, uncovered it, covered it. A silver light spilled across the lake.

She heard voices and saw Liz and Scott below her on the path. They were walking away from her, past the other houses on this side of the lake. She watched them. Only hours earlier, Liz had been here in the same place, also watching. Karen felt her face become like Liz's, calm, considering, watchful. No. She wasn't Liz. She thumped off the railing, knocked past the wicker table, and went inside, letting the screen door slam.

She was upstairs, taking a nap, when Liz came in. "Karen?" Liz bent over her, shaking her, her fingers digging into Karen's arm. "Wake up."

Karen sat up. Liz's face hovered over her, a round cheese, sharp cheese. Liz continued to shake her. Karen thought she might still be asleep, dreaming, mixing things up the way dreams did. Tobi would shake her, Tobi would dig into her flesh with hard fingers. Not Liz.

"Scott told me. He told me everything." Her freckles were like spots of light on her face.

"He told you?"

"That's what I said! He told me about you going to his place, he told me the whole thing. He told me everything."

"Why? Why'd he tell you?" Her toes throbbed as if someone had tramped on them, crushed them with hobnailed boots.

"I asked him. I knew something was wrong. I saw the way you two were acting. Do you think I'm utterly blind?"

Karen turned over and over in the bed.

"What did you think you were doing? Did you think at all? Did you think of anyone but yourself and your little adolescent crush? Do you know what you did? I mean, really did? You betrayed me."

Karen was shaking under the covers. She huddled into herself, knees pulled up, arms tight to her body.

Thirty-two

K aren Freed?" the voice on the phone said.
"Yes."

"This is Kevin Mason."

"I'm sorry, we don't buy anything over the phone."

"What? Oh, you think — I'm not a salesman. This is Kevin Mason."

"Who?"

"Kevin Mason," he said loudly.

"I'm not deaf," she said, sounding like her grandmother.

"What? Is this Karen Freed?"

"Yes!"

"Well," he said patiently, "this is Kevin Mason."

"I give up. Who are you?"

"You don't remember?"

He sounded so disappointed she hurried to reassure him. "Oh, sure, I just — you know, for a moment —"

"I've got your name here," he said. "The job's open. Do you want it?"

And finally she remembered. Kevin Mason. The tiny doughnut shop. The tall, skinny boy with the pimple tattoo.

She went down there the next day after school. "I called you first," Kevin Mason said. "Before anybody else on the list." What list? Karen wondered, remembering the scrap of paper he'd scribbled her name on. But it was nice of him. He was nice. He fixed her a cup of cocoa, added a sugar doughnut. "It's on the house." He told her about his new job, working night shift at the candle factory. "I get health insurance, I get paid more, I have a chance for advancement."

"I was just looking for summer work," she reminded him. "You're full-time, aren't you?"

"That's okay. They can find somebody else in the fall."

He asked her to come in a few afternoons a week for the next couple weeks so he could train her. Then she could go to work right after school was over. "And I'll come in and check up, every now and then, see how you're doing." He winked. "Maybe you'll give me a free doughnut."

Right after Kevin Mason called, she had two more calls for jobs. One was from someplace she'd forgotten she'd even left an application. The other was from Scott's friend, Mr. Anderson, at the The Green Market. "You've already got a job?" He sounded disappointed. "Well, if things don't work out, check in with me. I need someone who can take charge a little bit."

"Thank you. I'll do that." She hung up. Take charge a little bit? That was her? That was the impression he had of her? She liked that. Maybe

205

things were looking up. Maybe. And maybe not. It was good that she had a job, but not good enough to make her feel really good for very long. Ever since the weekend at the lake, it seemed to her that the whole family was in a terrible mood. Tense, disagreeable, snappy — or maybe it was just her.

She was depressed. Every little thing bothered her, irritated her, upset her too much. Every time she thought of that last afternoon at the lake, her chest tightened, she could hardly breathe. She was unhappy with herself, with the world, with everything around her. She even got depressed over an absurd thing like the clothes Mr. Radosh, the principal, was wearing one day. Checked green pants, violet shirt, preppy shoes. It seemed so bizarre to her, so sad.

One night she heard her parents hassling over something, she didn't know what, only heard their voices from their room. "Oh, you always —" That was her mother. And "Why don't you —" Her father. That was all, but enough to make her think the worst, that they were splitting up, getting a divorce.

That night was hot, stifling. She took her sleeping bag into the yard and unrolled it under the mulberry tree. In the middle of the night she dragged back in, scratching her neck, her face, her arms. The no-see-ums had arrived and feasted on her. In the morning her face was puffy with little red flecks; her neck was swollen to twice its usual size. She scratched and scratched. Her mother dabbed on a green lotion, zinc and something else. "If this stuff doesn't work, you might have to go see Richard."

"Who?"

"Richard. Dr. Richard."

"Mom, he's a pediatrician. A baby doctor! I will not go to a baby doctor!"

Her mother threw the cotton swab into the wastebasket. "All right. All right! What's the matter with everyone? I've never seen such a houseful of prima donnas."

"What's the matter with you and Dad?" Karen blurted. "I heard you fighting."

Her mother looked at her. "Is that what's upsetting you? Karen. People who live together fight. It's impossible to live with someone without fighting."

"Well, what was it about?"

"I don't think I want to discuss that with you."

"Fine!" She stormed out, knowing that she was being less than honest, using her parents' quarrel as an excuse to explode or cry. Either one would do. That was the way she felt most of the time lately — ready to cry or scream.

Later that day, she had a fight with Tobi over a pair of flowered ankle socks they both wanted from the clean laundry. Tobi said they were hers; Karen said no, they weren't, Tobi had given them to her. "I want to wear them," she said, although she didn't truly care. But something made her insist. "I am going to wear them, Tobi!"

Tobi shrugged and threw them at her. "You know, you can be a real spoiled brat."

Karen wore the socks and felt miserable. Tobi was right, she was selfish, self-centered, egocentric, more pig than person. She tore herself down. She couldn't, wouldn't, even try to defend herself against the charges. Guilty! What was it Liz had said? Did you never think of anyone or anything but your own little miserable, stupid, ridiculous, adolescent self? Something mild like that.

Liz didn't talk to her anymore. She had cut Karen off, cut her out of her life. She passed Karen on the stairs, or coming out of the bathroom, or up the steps with a distant look, without a word. She sat next to her at the dinner table and there was a space between them wider than the house. Liz's eyes never strayed her way. She never acknowledged anything Karen said. It was as if Karen no longer existed for her.

They had had fights now and then in the past, but not a lot, never a lot of fights, not like some sisters who went at each other like cats and dogs. Fight with Liz? Why would she want to do that? And Liz fight with her? For that matter, Liz fight with anybody? Liz was the famous family peacemaker. Fighting and Liz didn't go together, didn't make sense. Except that now it did — bad sense.

Karen moved around as if there were a paper bag over her head. Every morning when she woke up, she counted. Five days since Liz talked to me. Eight days. Nine. She didn't get used to it.

One afternoon, coming home from school, she saw Liz across the street. Without thinking, Karen waved. Liz kept walking. Karen's arm dropped, she sat down on the curb, stunned, as if someone had hit her on the head. A woman passed her, hunchbacked, gray-faced. She glanced at Karen, then came back. "What's the matter?"

Karen shook her head, mumbled, "I've had a terrible fight with my sister. . . ."

"Uh-huh, uh-huh. That hurts, doesn't it?" What was she, a witch, cackling in glee over Karen's misery? She squeezed Karen's shoulder, dug her fingers right in. "You'll make it up with her," she said. "Oh, yes, you will, don't shake your head. Your very own sister? Of course, you will." Her face, close to Karen's, showed a fringe of stiff whiskers on her chin.

Surprisingly, that cheered her up and she went home feeling momentarily better. But Liz was still not talking to her and nothing was as it had been. But who said it would be? Where did she get that idea? And was that what she was waiting for? Was that what she expected? For everything to go back to the way it had been?

That evening she and Tobi were in the living room. Tobi sat cross-legged on the window seat with an art book. Karen should have been studying, exams were coming at her fast, but she was leafing through a photography magazine. She looked for a long time at a picture of a house in winter: sagging roof, smoke rising from the chimney, blue hills of snow in the distance. A simple picture, full of the feeling of coldness and winter. She saw that compared to this picture, the ones she took were awful — silly, pretentious stuff.

She began to feel depressed again and turned on the tv. A rerun of M*A*S*H, Alan Alda picking up a surgical knife, making a joke that cracks up everyone except the guy lying on the operating table. She flipped the dial. A special on street people. Quick shot of a bag lady. Floppy brown shoes, a long brown man's coat, a soiled white kerchief tied under her chin.

She started crying. Again. I should stop, she thought, this is terrible.

"Karen?" Tobi said. "What's the matter?"

"I don't know . . . everything. Everything is awful. . . ."

"Is it that business with Scott?"

"What do you mean? What business?"

Tobi shrugged. "Oh, I know about it, Liz told me."

Karen's heart grabbed. "She told you? She told you, Tobi?"

"Whatever got into you? I never acted like that when I was your age."

The tears, the humiliating, satisfying, irresistible tears came again. She ran out of the room, ran out of the house, snorting and crying, her eyes puffed and sore. Who else had Liz told? Mom? Dad? Grandma? Did they all despise her now, the way Liz did?

Thirty-three

S he woke up sick. Her head hurt, she had no strength in her legs, she had a deep, chesty cough. Yes, oh healthy one. She and her boasting about never getting sick. Now she was getting paid back. Her father moved the tv into her room. Tobi brought her tissues and the baby cup with a soft boiled egg. Liz stayed away.

"You'll be okay?" her mother said, lingering in the doorway. "I hate to leave you alone, sweetie. Don't forget, call me if you need me." They all left for school and work. She watched tv all day. Game shows. Soaps. Movies. The last movie she watched was called *The Game of Honor*. It was about a young girl and an older man. Don't look, she told herself. Don't watch it. Turn it off.

The man is a lawyer. Big office. Important clients. The girl is an honor student, beautiful, smart, editor of her high school paper. She prints an article her principal objects to. (This principal wears three-piece suits and a blow-dried haircut.) He censors the article. The girl is outraged; this is a violation of freedom of the press. Everyone tells her to forget it. She looks in the phone book, picks out a lawyer's name at random. She goes to see him, but at first he doesn't take her seriously. She persists, impressing him with her brains and beauty. Her nickname is Randy and she makes uneasy, but sophisticated, jokes about her name. He says, No, I will call you Miranda. It's easy to see he's on his way to being totally zapped by her.

His name is William. He's handsome, in an older-man way, sort of thin and fit. He jogs. He has a wife and children, he has a beautiful house, but he's not happy. He and his wife are having trouble. Bla bla bla bla bla. Finally, he goes to Randy's house. Her parents were conveniently away. They make love on the living room couch. William says, I love you. Randy says, I love you.

Next, they're romping around on a beach, little skimpy bathing suits, sun, sand. After that, racing each other down a footpath, jeans, sweat shirts, a breeze in the trees. Then they're at the zoo together; she's wearing something preppy, he's casual and well-pressed. The monkeys perform for them. After that, a whole bunch of scenes where they smile a lot (Randy and William, not the monkeys), say clever things, and tear off each other's clothes every chance they have.

In between all this, they have terrific battles with the school board and the principal. He makes great speeches. She makes great speeches. He tells her she should be a lawyer. They win their case. The school paper will not be censored. Anyway, school is over. It's summer. He's still unhappy. They keep seeing each other. Once or twice he says something about being too old for her. But she always puts her perfect little fingers over his mouth and tears off her clothes and tears off his clothes and they make love and everything is wonderful.

Then one day he's with Randy and who comes into the restaurant but his wife! She sits down. She's not so bad-looking. She's actually rather nice. They all talk about the case. William's wife knows all about it. Randy is sweet — but young. Suddenly you can see how young she is, and you can see William seeing how young she is. Or maybe how old he is. Or maybe how nice his wife is. And what a fool he is. So then he's in the park with Randy again, telling her, I'm too old for you. He's sober and brave and so is she, although they both cry and say good-bye oh good-bye good-bye, and creep off into the bushes to make love one last time.

And that's that.

Except for one final scene when she passes his office, looks up at the window, and you can see on her face how she's still heartbroken, but you also notice even more how gorgeous she is and how, even though she's still thinking about William practically every minute, other men can't keep their eyes off her. She walks down the street. You know she'll be okay.

"Good movie?" Her father looked in. Behind him, Liz passed, giving her father a little affectionate pat.

Karen shook her head.

"Oh, sorry about that."

She coughed. Her eyes teared, her nose ran.

"Anyway, sometimes it's fun to watch a really bad movie."

213

"Sure," she said.

That night, she woke up coughing uncontrollably. She hung over the side of the bed, coughing and spitting into tissues. She was dying. Spitting out her life's blood. They all knew she was dying, and even so, Liz wouldn't forgive her, and none of them cared. She coughed and spit and cried.

Thirty-four

K aren. Over here." Scott was parked in his truck at the corner. At the sight of him, her stomach climbed straight up into her throat, nauseating her. It was the first time she'd seen him since the lake.

She walked toward him.

"Hello, Karen." A brief smile flickered under his mustache. That was new. "I'd like to talk to you," he said, opening the passenger door. "Please." She shrugged and climbed into the truck. He pulled away from the curb. She looked out the window; the sky was blue, perfectly blue, like an egg.

"So, how've you been?" he said.

"Terrific." He missed the irony, of course. "You've got a mustache."

He fingered the silky growth. "I wanted a change."

He drove across town; the streets were dry and bare; a man sat in a window, knees up, a woman languidly entered a bar. They drove over railroad tracks, rusted and broken, past a used car lot, flags waving limply. It was still too hot for June. "Where are you going?" she asked.

"I have to drop some plans off. Kitchen remodeling job." He stopped at an old, impressive-looking house on Valley Drive. "I'll just be a minute." The plans were rolled up in a tube.

When he came back, he said, "You want something? Ice cream?"

"No."

"A beer would be nice now." He pulled into the parking lot of a red and white diner in the shape of a hot dog. There was a red-and-white sign over the burning tin roof. FRANK'S HOT DOGS AND FRIES. SOFT ICE CREAM. "Sure about the ice cream?"

"Is this what you want to talk to me about?"

"Karen, you've changed."

"Have I?" She was lightheaded, felt almost sick again. A scrap of dream from last night came back to her, something about the mulberry tree, Liz and she sitting together. The dream had been soft, windy, warm, private. Why think of it now? The truck was dry, harsh, flat, hot.

Scott lit a cigarette. "Tell me, how's Liz?"

"Why don't you ask her?" She put her head back against the seat.

"She's not — we're not on very good terms right now." He stared out the window, coughed, pulled at his shirt. "That's putting it mildly. She won't see me. I was wondering — would you talk to her?"

Karen looked at him disbelievingly. "You want me to talk to Liz for you? Me, put in a good word for you?"

"Something like that."

"That's sort of funny."

216

He tapped ash over the window. "You know, you could just tell her that what happened was not so important. Just one of those things, it didn't mean anything. It's the sort of thing — the sort of thing that can happen. It can happen to a man. It can happen."

She was startled by a desire to hit him in the face. "I want to get out of here," she said. "I want to get out of this truck."

"What's the matter? Wait —"

She opened the door, jumped out, stumbled; she'd worn high-heeled, cork-soled sandals to school. She should have worn sneakers. If she'd known what was coming, she would have worn her running sneakers and her boxing gloves, too.

Scott came after her. "Karen, what's happening, where are you going?" He caught her arm.

"Go away. Leave me alone! Speak to Liz yourself! I'm not saying anything for you. Nothing!" His hand on her arm made her shudder.

"All right." He put up his hands. "If that's the way it is — I'll drive you home. Do you even know where you are?"

"Go *away*."

"Hey." He half-smiled under his new, soft little mustache. "You know, you always say that when you see me lately."

She turned on him, beating on him with her fists, pounding and hitting, wanting to hurt. She punched him in the chest, his belly, tried to hit him in the face.

He flung up his hands, fended her off. "Okay! Okay! Stop it!" He shoved her away. "That's enough!" They stared at each other.

"Did I hurt you?" she said.

He shrugged.

"Did I *hurt* you?"

"You're strong."

"I wanted to hurt you."

"You don't have to hate me so much, Karen."

She didn't answer. What was the point? What could she say, anyway? Maybe I won't hate you someday, Scott, but right now, I do — and I have to.

Thirty-five

Over the weekend, her parents flew to Atlantic City for a dental convention. They left Friday night and wouldn't return until Tuesday. Of course Karen had been alone with her sisters before, but never like this. The house was quiet, too quiet. It wasn't just her parents being away. It was she and Liz and Tobi, each in her own room: separated, alone. Each going her own way. She and Liz — so much distance between them. They were like two particles of dust floating in a vast space, never touching, never making contact.

In the morning she pulled on shorts, a T-shirt, cleaned her teeth, brushed her hair, barefooted it past her sisters' doors. Quiet. Everything so quiet. She took in the newspaper, spread it out on the kitchen table. Her horoscope said, "You have troubles. Don't keep them to yourself. Talk them over with someone you trust." Who would that be?

Liz, I'm troubled.

Silence.

I made a mistake and I did something that was rash, no it was stupid, the whole thing with Scott. . . .

Silence.

Well, maybe stupid and rash don't cover it. Deluded? I was in love with him — had a crush on him; I didn't think it was puppy love and if you want to know the truth, I still don't.

Silence.

I haven't got it all figured out; can you love someone and hate him at the same time? I read that once in a book; I never understood it, but now I do.

Silence.

In fact, right now, I feel like I love you and hate you at the same time.

Silence.

Can't you say something?

Silence.

Okay, you were right in what you said about me; it's true I didn't think of you. Or — maybe I did and I was jealous, wanted what you had. I don't mean just Scott . . . more than that. Your life, your assurance, your beauty. I know it's crazy!

Silence.

And I let myself believe Scott loved me, too. Does that make you angry?

Silence.

Anyway, I was wrong about Scott.

Silence.

Are you ever going to speak to me again, Liz?

Silence.

She went outside and picked dandelions. She put them in a jar, set it on the dining room table. She set the table with three place mats, cloth napkins

220

in the wooden napkin rings, a pitcher of milk, the bread in a basket. Tobi came down and whistled approvingly. Liz said nothing.

Later, her grandmother called to see how they were doing. "How are you? How are your sisters?"

"Fine, Grandma."

"What's Liz doing?"

"Right now? Laundry, I think."

"Poetry is a dead end. She needs a profession. Let me say hello to Tobi."

"She went out running, Grandma."

"Is she with that man? Tell her to call me when she comes home."

In the afternoon Karen shopped at the market, bought paper towels, butter, milk, a quart of the first New Jersey strawberries. Liz adored strawberries. For supper, she made meat loaf, baked potatoes, a big green salad. She set the table again in the dining room. Strawberries and cream for dessert. "I'm stuffing myself," Tobi said, having put a piece of meat loaf big enough for a mouse on her plate.

Liz said nothing. Not to Karen. Then Karen didn't want to eat. She left the table. "Where're you going?" Tobi said. In the living room she curled up on the window seat. She heard Liz and Tobi talking about Tobi's new summer job in an old people's home. "One of the residents came over to me, Mr. Adler, he's ninety-six. I was picking up breakfast trays, he trots into a room and brings out the tray for me, like I might wear myself out, you know?" Tobi and Liz laughed. "Then he says, 'Now don't take this wrong, sweetheart, but I used to have a girl friend who looked just like you.' And then, Liz, he

221

wriggled his eyebrows at me, like woo! woo! honey!"

The sound of their laughter hurt Karen. Sisterly, funny, affectionate, warm laughter. Liz had everything for Tobi, nothing for her. All the things she'd done today, from picking the dandelions to baking the meat loaf, all had been for Liz. She had been courting her, seeking her approval, waiting for her to see her again and to say — what? Something. Anything. Even her name! *Karen. Hello, Karen. Hi, Karen. Oh, there you are, Karen.*

Yes, here she was! She was here, wasn't she? She was living, she was breathing, she was Liz's sister, too! Had been for almost sixteen years. Did Liz think she'd blotted Karen out forever? Liz's hardness stunned her. She thought of the paper cutouts she used to make when she was a kid. Fold paper, cut, unfold. Stars. Snowflakes. Diamonds. The hardest to do was the doll series with linked hands. She learned how to do it. It was her favorite. She always had one of the doll cutouts pasted on her window. But when Tobi was angry at her, she'd come into Karen's room and snip through the clasped hands, ruining her cutout. Snip. Snip. Snip. And the paper dolls would fall, one by one, to the floor.

Sunday morning, Tobi went out early. "I may or may not be back tonight." Liz was in her room, door closed; that meant she was writing.

Their grandmother called again. "Years ago, women didn't go away and leave their families for days on end. It's all this liberated nonsense."

"Grandma, you ran a business."

"I never neglected and deserted my family."

"Mom and Dad are coming back on Tuesday, Grandma."

"I admire your loyalty, Karen. You come by that quality honestly from your father. He laughs and smiles, but I know life is a disappointment to him."

"It is?"

"I'm coming over to cook for you," she said.

"You're going to drive, Grandma?"

"I'm perfectly capable, Karen. The Austin needs an outing, anyway."

She arrived about an hour later, looked pityingly at Karen for a moment, then began cooking as if they were starving Ethiopians. She wore a long, green, linen apron over her dress. Karen was appointed her chief assistant; at her grandmother's direction she cut, peeled, scraped, and fetched. Her grandmother made enough food for weeks, for months, possibly for years. A large pot of stuffed cabbage, dozens of coconut cookies, two apple strudels, a noodle pudding with cheese and raisins, and a chocolate cake whose aroma filled the house for hours.

After her grandmother left, the house was silent. Liz and Karen were in the house, but it was silent. Karen walked restlessly down the stairs, up the stairs, down the stairs, up the stairs. Go out, she told herself. Mow the lawn. If you're going to stay in, wash the dishes. Study for the exams. Call Marisa. Do something. Tobi used to keep gerbils; they would tread their wheels endlessly, squeaking and treading and getting nowhere. Up and down the stairs Karen went, a human gerbil.

The phone rang. "Karen — it's me, Tobi. Come get me."

"What's the matter? Where are you?"

"Tell Liz to come get me. I'm in a phone booth without my shoes."

Thirty-six

Liz jammed on the brakes. Usually she was tolerant and kind behind the wheel. Now she hunched, muttering curses at the slowness and stupidity of other drivers. To the rescue of Tobi. And what about Karen? Didn't she need rescuing, too? This silence between them was filling her lungs, drowning her.

"Tobi said the corner of Weaver and —"

"Weaver and Gracey," Karen said.

"A telephone booth? Are you sure you heard right?"

"Yes. And no shoes."

"What else did she say?"

"I told you everything, Liz. She said to come get her."

"Did she sound all right; I mean, like it was *funny* she had no shoes, or —?"

"No. She sounded upset."

Karen leaned back against the seat. So they were talking again — sort of, but only because of Tobi.

What happened after they got Tobi? Would the silence fall again? Maybe Liz would only talk to her in emergencies. A broken leg would be worth a line or two. A heart attack would give her a paragraph's worth of conversation. If somebody died, Liz might talk to her for fifteen minutes.

"I saw Scott the other day. He asked me to talk to you."

"You, of all people —"

"Right. That's what I said. Do you think you'll make up with him?"

"I don't know."

"Maybe you should."

Liz glanced at her briefly. "Advice?"

"No!" Karen flushed.

There was a long silence, then Liz said, "I'll just have to wait and see what happens. I trusted Scott."

"He said — he asked me to tell you it was just something that happens to a man sometimes." She hated saying it. She slouched down in the seat, her head burning.

"I know. I know all that! But what about the real thing? Trust," Liz repeated. "Take Mom and Dad — whatever their problems are, they know they can trust each other. It's not something they click on and off." Her voice got choked. "I always thought Scott was the nicest man I'd ever met."

Karen looked out the window. Why didn't Liz just say it? She had ruined Liz's life. "Do you want to hit me?" she blurted.

"No, I don't want to hit you!"

"Go ahead, do it. I give you permission. Hit me!"

"Stop that, Karen."

"If it'll make you feel better —"

226

"It isn't that simple."

"I wish it was! I wish it was, Liz!"

Liz glanced at her, her freckles bright, then her eyes slid past Karen. "There she is. There's Tobi!"

Tobi was leaning against a phone booth, standing on one foot. Karen got out to let her sit in the front seat. There were big purple bruises on Tobi's arms. "Did Jason do that, Tobi?" She couldn't believe it. She wanted to jump out of the car and kill him.

"He was drinking," Tobi said. "He loses his head when he drinks. He grabbed me. And then he hid my shoes so I couldn't leave." She started to laugh, then turned her head and sobbed.

"Oh, god, Tobes —" Karen reached over the seat to hug her. Then Liz was hugging her, too, the three of them tangled up, all of them crying.

At home, they put ice on Tobi's arms, fussed over her, bringing her food and combing her hair and petting her. When she thought of Jason hiding her shoes, Tobi would laugh, and then cry and then laugh again. Finally she calmed down. "I don't want Mom and Dad to know."

"Tobi," Liz said, "it's no good. He's not right. You know Dad never lifted a finger to one of us —"

Tobi sniffed. "Dad — any one of us could beat him up."

Later, Liz went out to the store to buy a few things. "I don't think we should leave Tobi alone," she said to Karen.

"I'll stay with her. Wait. Liz, wait." She put out her hands. "What about us?"

"What about us?" Liz said.

"I don't want — You haven't talked to me in weeks!"

"I'm talking now."

"Because of Tobi! What happens tomorrow?"

Liz hesitated. "I don't know," she said. "I guess we'll talk tomorrow, too."

"Liz! —"

Liz picked up her car keys. "I don't think everything can be spelled out, Karen. Maybe we just have to wait and see."

Tobi and Karen were upstairs in Tobi's room when they heard a tremendous banging on the front door.

"It's Jason," Tobi said. "I don't want to talk to him!"

"I'll get it," Karen said. She opened the front door. There was Jason, the awful man, big as ever, a kind of slipping, sliding smile coming and going on his face. "Where's my girl? Where's Tobi?"

From the top of the stairs, Tobi screamed, "Go home, Jason. How dare you follow me here!" She went into her room, slammed her door, and locked it — you could hear the lock clicking.

Jason looked past Karen, into the house, with a puddled, sad-eyed expression. Was he drunk? Half drunk? On the way to being sober? Safe? Dangerous? She'd never been alone with a drunken man. She was scared and thought about locking herself in her room, too. Then she got mad. This was her house. "Tobi wants you to leave, and so do I." Her knees were shaking.

His eyes focused on her. Then, as meekly as could be, he said, "Would you give me a cup of coffee, please?"

"Outside," she said. "You stay outside." She closed the door on him and peeked through the little side window. He sat down on the steps, his hands folded in his lap. As Grandma would have said, Looking like butter would melt in his mouth.

She heated up Liz's morning coffee and brought him out a cup. "Thank you." He lifted the cup to his lips as delicately as if he were at a tea party. If Karen hadn't been remembering the bruises on Tobi's arms every minute, it might have been funny.

He started telling her how much he loved Tobi and how sorry he was and how he was going to change. She didn't say anything. She wished he'd finish his coffee and go. Even though he was so mild, she didn't trust him. "Will you ask Tobi to come down and talk to me? Will you just ask her that? Then I'll go."

What was this — was she everyone's go-between? Speak to Liz. Ask Tobi. A pox on all of them! She went upstairs. "He wants to see you."

"No," Tobi said. "I know him. I'll go down and then he'll start crying, and I'll say, Okay, okay, all is forgiven. No. Let him suffer a little!" She walked up and down her room, her arms wrapped around herself. "Is he suffering?"

"I don't know. He seems sorry."

"Not good enough. I'm not going through life with purple arms." She went to the window. "God. Everything is so complicated. I wish I didn't love him."

Karen went back downstairs. "She doesn't want to talk to you," she said, standing in the doorway.

"Did you tell her —" Jason began in a humble voice.

"I told her. You have to go. Now."

"I could just wait here —"

"No." Her voice was not exactly loud, but it was strong; it reminded her of her grandmother's voice. "You have to go," she repeated. "Right now."

She watched until he got in his car and drove off.

"Is he gone? Did you get rid of him?" Tobi leaned over the banister.

"He's gone," Karen said, going up the stairs.

"Good. You did good, Karen." Tobi hugged her, then ran down the hall, calling, "I have to pee! I've been holding it, I didn't dare even pee when he was here!"

Karen went to her room and took Scott's T-shirts, the two guilty secrets, off the shelf. She didn't even want to touch them. She dropped them on the floor, then kicked the one that had been Liz's down the hall into Liz's room. She had to pick it up to put it back in Liz's bureau.

In her room again, she looked down at the T-shirt she'd worn home from Scott's apartment. What was she to do with that one? Run it up a flagpole and give it the Bronx cheer? Wrap it around her head as a sweatband? Rip it up for rags? That appealed to her — the closest she'd ever get to mopping up the floor with Scott. She ripped it apart. "All right," she said, out loud, "that's taken care of." And heard again her grandmother's voice lodged in her throat.

"Did you say something?" Tobi asked, poking in her head.

"I have a lot of things to say," Karen said.

"Oh, my." Tobi raised her eyebrows mockingly. They linked arms and went downstairs. A few moments later, Liz came back with a grocery bag. "You guys hungry? If you make cheese sandwiches, Tobi,

I'll make some chocolate pudding." She hesitated, then touched Karen's arm. "Want to set the table?"

Karen opened the silverware drawer, then reached past Liz for the napkins. Her arm brushed Liz's. Another touch. Soon they'd sit down and eat together. It seemed like two tremendous steps.

She got the blue plates with the hand-painted sunflowers in the middle down from the top shelf, where her mother had banished them because they were all chipped. It was true, there was hardly an untouched, smooth edge to a single plate. But she'd always loved them. Who cared about a few chips? The blue was vivid as sky, the gold of the sunflower drew you into its warm center.

The cheese sandwiches were ready before the chocolate pudding. They were all ravenous. They sat around the kitchen table, eating the sandwiches and drinking glass after glass of cold milk.

About the Author

Norma Fox Mazer is the author of thirteen books for young readers, among them *Taking Terri Mueller, When We First Met,* and *Downtown.* Ms. Mazer has twice won the Lewis Carroll Shelf Award; she has also won the California Young Readers' Medal and has been nominated for the National Book Award.

Ms. Mazer says, "I am one of three sisters and I have three daughters. So it was a very natural thing for me to write a book about three sisters. I grew up a middle sister, and I've always had a lot of sympathy for any middle sister.... But when I began to write about Liz, Tobi, and Karen, it was Karen, the youngest sister, whose story I wanted to tell." Ms. Mazer and her husband, Harry Mazer, live in the Pompey Hills outside Syracuse, New York.